Death Comes Scampering

by

Peter Chegwidden

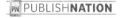

www.publishnation.co.uk

Chapter One

Edith Footlong read the notice from the DWP confirming her state pension and gazed out of the kitchen window. Retirement. Widowhood and retirement. Reg had departed about three years before, passing away peacefully in his sleep, the best way to leave this life for the next Edith considered. And now she was retired as well as being alone.

Friends who had retired joked that she'd be busier than she'd ever been, and would wonder where she found the time to go to work. Just at the moment it didn't feel like that.

But she was grateful for the many friends she had. She was grateful for her family but her own children had emigrated, Peter to Matamata in New Zealand, Kathleen to the U.S.A., Woodford in California to be precise. So she saw precious little of them.

Shortly after her husband died the covid pandemic fell upon the world and many things changed, but at least she'd avoided catching it and had been given three jabs to help protect her. That was quite enough jabs, she'd decided, although she knew there would be a booster later in the year and it probably wouldn't end there. Human pin-cushions we are, she thought. To add to her current misery there was now a July heatwave to welcome her to retirement. She'd remember 2022 that was for sure, and that was without the one matter that lay ahead that she didn't yet know about that would make certain she didn't forget it.

***

The village where Edith lived stood above the Kent Downs, seemingly teetering on the edge in its lofty position from whence a long descent southwards cascaded into the valley beyond. In the valley ran the stream known as the river Len on its way to the mighty Medway which it joined in Maidstone, Kent's county town. In this valley were truly rustic idylls, beautiful rolling countryside, delightful views, peace and tranquillity, yet humans had done much to despoil it and ruin it. For here too was the high speed rail link, the M20 motorway, and even the often overcrowded A20 en route from Maidstone to Ashford. To say nothing of rampant house-building in the area.

But the village of Little Scampering rested above it all and feasted on the views whilst managing to ignore the worst aspects, confirmation indeed that much of Kent remains rural and in many parts astoundingly lovely. Little Scampering was largely unaffected by housing development which may have been due to its geographical position, poor road access and being within the Kent Downs AONB.

Edith had been born and bred here but had lived most of her life in Bearsted, east of Maidstone, where she and Reg had raised their two children, a location better suited to Reg's daily commute to London and for the schools of course. When the children became teenagers she started a small part-time job in a local undertakers which conveniently became full-time when the offspring had sorted out their own careers and marriages.

As the business grew (growth industry, Edith reasoned, catering for the dead) she took on a more senior position, one that she kept until retirement.

Reg came from Minster on the isle of Sheppey and they met by chance on the seafront there. It was almost Edith's last day on earth, for, unseen by her parents, she got into difficulties while bathing and Reg came to her rescue, taking advantage of the situation to administer the kiss-of-life when there was actually no medical need. They married two years later and lived in Sittingbourne until Reg made his own mark in the world of insurance and they were able to move on.

Little Scampering resided south of Sittingbourne, roughly north of Hollingbourne, Harrietsham, and Lenham, and remained pleasantly remote enough. Edith came back there with her husband in 2016, to what they hoped would be their retirement home. Sadly poor Reg never actually retired, dying within sight of the event. So near and yet so far.

**

Little Scampering has no claims to fame, no church and no shop, the village emporium closing back in 1992. The pub, the *Downsman*, has just about managed to survive thanks to an entrepreneurial landlord and an even more entrepreneurial landlord's wife. There is a number of buildings of various ages, scattered along a meandering lane beset with some of the finest examples of Kentish potholes, and Edith occupies one of these buildings, a detached cottage which she had named *Bienvenue a la Maison*, mainly because she thought it sounded better than 'welcome home', and not because she was acquainted with France or the French language.

Some villagers know each other and most are content with their lot and with living in this sleepy hamlet. However, Little Scampering is about to impact on their lives in a way they would rather have avoided if at all possible.

Chapter Two

Carl and Alana Merde had moved to Little Scampering to escape to the country, leaving their flat in Eltham behind them, and had dwelled here for four years, both loving the southern aspect rear garden where they could sit out in whatever sunshine was granted them. And July 2022 brought them sunshine beyond their wildest dreams. While some villagers took shelter from the intense heat Carl and Alana laid out on their patio under their sun umbrellas and did very little else at all. That is, until the fateful day.

There was no question about the murder weapon. It was still in situ. 75-year-old Alana Merde was lying flat on the patio, spreadeagled, with the large kitchen knife sticking out of her chest.

Her husband, 78-year-old Carl, had found her about 5.40 that morning and he appeared anything but distraught and heartbroken, although perhaps the shock hadn't set it. The doctor was being annoyingly vague, that is, annoying to an impatient DCI Sheelagh Mehedren, and suggested time of death to be 'the early hours', maybe between 1 a.m. and 3 a.m.

Carl told the DCI he'd been to the toilet about 2.30 and his wife had been tucked up in bed 'snoring her head off' at that stage, so the murder must've taken place a short while after that. However, that was assuming he was telling the truth, and to Sheelagh he was already top of a list of one when it came to suspects. A quick check showed that, curiously, the side gate was unbolted so that did provide an access point to the rear of their semi-detached property.

As was her wont the DCI tapped her teeth with her pen as she looked all around her and pondered the situation. If it wasn't Carl how was Alana lured out onto the patio, without disturbing her husband? Presumably she finished up face to face with her killer, yet was there something odd about how she'd ended up, so perfectly spreadeagled? Surely you would stagger backwards and crumple in some kind of heap. Maybe the assassin arranged her like that after slaying her.

Was it significant? Perhaps. One thing was certain, their chances of finding any prints on the knife were zero, unless the offender was seriously careless, so there probably wouldn't be any of value elsewhere. But hey-ho, time would tell.

"Don't suppose Mr Merde could rustle up a bacon sandwich, Willie? I'm famished." DS Willie Broughton gave his boss a sideways look bordering on contempt. "No, I suppose not," she concluded. Willie chuckled. "He doesn't seem all that bothered, does he Willie?"

"Stunned I expect ma'am. Finding your life partner murdered like that must do all sorts of things to the mind. Anyway, there are two sons, Albert and Stephen. They've been informed and are heading this way to take care of dad."

"Albert? Old is he?"

"No idea. Why?"

"Don't get many of the younger generations named Albert. Bit old fashioned."

"Never bothered to ask why I was called Willoughby. Perhaps I was conceived in a caravan…."

"Talking of which," Sheelagh continued, ignoring her DS, "the doc says no obvious signs of anything sexual but the post mortem will reveal all, of course. She's just wearing a flimsy nightie and that looks as if it's been nicely arranged. No signs of any other kind of assault, other than the stabbing. Carl Merde is still my number one target but must keep an open mind."

"Just wearing is about right, ma'am. That's almost baby-doll stuff…."

"You're too young to be thinking about such things, sunshine. Now, are we knocking up all the neighbours?"

"Yes ma'am, a rude awakening for a few, but the presence of emergency vehicles arriving sirens sounding, blue lights flashing has aroused the rest I can assure you!"

***

Edith was one of the neighbours being 'knocked up'. *Bienvenue* was some distance away from the unnamed cottage where Mrs Merde had met her end and consequently she'd been restricted to briefly passing the time of day on the odd occasion

5

she met either Carl or Alana. She knew they'd moved from south-east London but otherwise knew very little about them beyond being aware they'd upset their immediate neighbours as well as the elderly Mrs Cathcart since their arrival. Grace Cathcart had complained about Carl's unnecessary use of obnoxious language in public and Edith didn't doubt others were offended by it but chose not to mention it. She'd never heard him herself so kept an open mind.

Grace, like Edith, had been born in Little Scampering but had lived there her whole life, and was not keen on incomers, least of all those who were escaping the big towns and cities and brought their unpleasant urban manners with them.

DC Sian Stramer was covering the properties at the southern end of the village in the company of rookie PC Thomas Bowlman, who looked far too young to be a policeman or to occupy any position of authority. But he was keen and determined and Sian had a good, instinctive feeling about him and his likely progression in the force. Also with them was PC Emily Coombes, a no-nonsense officer with considerable experience, and Sian sent her alone to one side of the road while she and Thomas tackled the other.

Thus it was that they came upon *Bienvenue*.

***

"Edith Veronica Margaret Footlong," she revealed in answer to Sian's question, unnecessarily adding her two middle forenames, both of which were omitted in the Detective Constable's notes.

Edith found herself thinking that the uniformed officer standing next to her inquisitor on the doorstep ought to be in school being too young to be at work. She mused on the fact that when she was a child police officers looked at least ten feet tall whereas this one was nearer the ground than she was at five feet nine. Rather than up, she was looking down.

Sian Stramer first established if Carl and Alana Merde were well known to Edith, that is, if they were very close friends, or if they were merely acquaintances, or just neighbours. This helped determine the way she tackled handling the despatch of the news,

6

and was relieved to learn they were regarded as just fellow villagers.

The sad information imparted did not appear to shock Edith which was, in some respects, rather surprising. But Edith, having worked for a funeral director, was seeing business potential in the matter instead of visualising the dreadful scene of the death. Of course, Sian could reveal very little, confining herself to the fact Alana Merde had been found dead in possibly suspicious circumstances. Mrs Footlong would've liked all the details, none of which the police were prepared to divulge or comment upon.

In fact, Thomas Bowlman was taken aback by the lady's unfeeling approach, which he mentioned to Sian as soon as they'd left.

"It's like that, Thomas," she explained, "they get all excited, like, when they ought to be collapsing in a chair shocked by what they've heard. Didn't she just want to know all the ins and outs even when I'd already said we could say no more! Ghoulish, if you ask me. Okay, let's try next door."

The two officers managed to glean that Edith had seen nothing unusual, that she didn't know much about Mr and Mrs Merde, but would let them know if she learned or remembered anything! Sian and Thomas blamed it on too much TV crime.

The lane through the village was now closed and the properties close to the scene of the crime were incorporated into a taped-off area. Neighbour started visiting neighbour and where it was not possible the telephone was used. Within half an hour Edith was hosting a kind of afterwards-at, providing tea and biscuits quite happily for six villagers who congregated outside and were subsequently invited in.

And in due course Little Scampering was invaded by the media.

***

By that time Edith's party had broken up, but she had kept her ears open and had indeed learned more of Mr and Mrs Merde. Firstly, they pronounced their surname 'Merd' which was hardly surprising, even more so now in their revised circumstances. Said as written Merde might've sounded like 'murder'. Most inappropriate! However, she decided she would write things down, at this stage just in case they might prove important to the police, and found a suitable notebook which she headed up "Little Scampering Unexplained Death" and into which she penned all she had chanced upon.

In the absence of more detailed information from the police her neighbours had come to the conclusion that "suspicious death" actually meant Mr Merde must've killed Mrs Merde, and then they set about deciding on the means of death, suggestions ranging from strangulation to hitting her over the head, from smothering her with a pillow to stabbing her. It was a natural progression from that to debating how it came about and how the attack took place, each person demonstrating a vivid imagination that seemed curiously out of place in the presence of the death of a neighbour.

Edith sat quietly and contemplated the whole affair and people's reactions. No sadness had been expressed, no sympathy for the grieving husband (who had been roundly condemned instead), no thoughts for the serious nature of what might prove to be a serious crime. And if indeed it was murder suppose Carl Merde wasn't responsible? Was it he who discovered the body? What a dreadful way to find your spouse.

And so Edith's inquisitive mind starting probing. Writings in the notebook were expanded. She listed her six guests and attributed comments to each, as far as she could recall them, and set aside a page headed 'Conclusions'. One of the first entries on this page was the fact that nobody had a good word for Mr and Mrs Merde, despite the truth that all six neighbours weren't speaking from personal experience, or so they said.

Hearsay was rampant. She read through all she had written and discovered she was longing to find out exactly what Alana and Carl were actually like, and what villagers who really did know them thought of them. She'd call on Grace Cathcart. She had never been convinced Grace had heard Mr Merde use bad language in the road and decided she too might've been acting on rumour.

"Actually," she said out loud to herself, "I know nothing about them, and now I'm curious."

8

Chapter Three

Media representatives found nothing but hearsay and rumour, very little of which was of any value until the police revealed more, and they did not tarry long. Some residents of Little Scampering were keen to talk, possibly in the hope of getting their pictures in the papers or, better still, on TV. But there was so little substance to their stories that they were politely ignored for the most part.

The police had carted the poor widower off to the station to be questioned and he didn't seem to mind a bit. DCI Sheelagh Mehedren, a woman of strength, cutting comment and general impatience, was capable of being extremely compassionate when the occasion demanded, and was prepared to offer a degree to comfort to Carl Merde despite being convinced he was the killer. Seriously, she thought, could it really be anyone else?

She acted with a kindness she didn't feel when interviewing Mr Merde, speaking quietly and with the gentlest of voices. DS Willoughby "Willie" Broughton sat silently observing Carl's reactions of which there were precious few. He stuck to his story, but one important image was emerging that both officers picked up on. He didn't seem to be grieving and that was perhaps explained by the shock, the harsh reality that hadn't hit home yet, the realisation his wife had been killed, and that he'd discovered the body, a horrible and unthinkable situation for any human to be faced with.

But....

Sheelagh pressed on, and gradually Carl opened up on his relationship with Alana and in so doing so placed himself firmly in the frame for the crime. The DCI had the ability to probe in this manner, an aspect of her skill that Willie marvelled at and hoped he could learn by working with her. He'd once asked, tongue in cheek, why she was so clever. She'd replied that she was a woman, which gave her an advantage over Willie, and was a DCI which meant she was right even when she was wrong. He didn't ask any more questions.

"When we met," Carl revealed, "she was my princess and I'd have done anything for her. She was everything I wanted in a woman and I couldn't believe my luck. She was a princess in those days. A very beautiful girl, and the blokes were so jealous of me, were they ever! I'd won a precious prize, that's for sure. I was so in love I did everything she asked of me. I worshipped her, you see, just worshipped her.

"We had our two boys. She never went to work. I was a carpenter and worked all hours and then came home and had to look after the kids while she did sod all. And still I worshipped her, fool that I was. And in time I got fed up with it, realised I'd been taken in, but it was too late. I was her slave. She said jump and I'd ask how many hoops. So I got resentful but what good does it do you, I ask you?

"Even when we moved to Little Scampering and she upset the neighbours, on one side, and it was left to me to annoy them just to please her! Weak little excuse for a man I was." Sheelagh interrupted.

"Which neighbours, Carl?"

"Oh, them, Wally and Beryl, Castle Cottage."

"What upset them, Carl?"

"Complained about the noise, just because our family used to come down, sit outside, and enjoy themselves, y'know, just being happy, know what I mean."

"They complained about that?"

"No, not exactly. Didn't actually ever complain. Just made comments like 'we've had it quiet too long' and that sort of thing. I refused to speak to them to please Alana, but she used to talk to them, mainly to be nasty so that was alright, and then we didn't speak to them at all, except when I made sarky and offensive remarks, and that made Alana happy. I did it for her, and hoped I'd pleased her. They were nasty neighbours, know what I mean."

Sheelagh had a feeling she knew exactly what Carl meant, and wondered who was actually the nastier neighbours.

***

Edith had bumped into Felicity Trumpling, wife of the *Downsman's* landlord, Eric. They had suffered a difficult ride during the pandemic, having to close the pub at first, and then find lots of interesting ways to benefit from the easing of restrictions. A take-away service, expanded to fish-and-chips, and then a home delivery arrangement, meant that they'd ridden out the storm, and it was widely rumoured to be Felicity's driving force that had produced results.

Reg and Edith had been frequent visitors to the *Downsman* before the pandemic, Reg loving a pint or three, not that Edith drank much and had not been seen in the pub since his death.

"Hello Edith, bad business that, eh? Reckon old Carl did his wife in, what have you heard?"

"Well, Alana's dead and foul play is suspected, but that doesn't mean Carl had a hand in it."

"Didn't he?" Felicity winked, "Well, I'll tell you, if you ask me, he couldn't wait to be shot of her, they used to row like nobody's business. Had a few bust ups in the pub, you know! Stories I could tell, stories I could tell. Told that girl from the local paper but strangely she didn't seem very interested. Shame. Hoped to get a bit of publicity for the pub."

"I don't like the idea of married couples arguing in public myself ….."

"Oh, you'd love it. 'Course the drink makes it worse. Some of it's so petty and trivial you can't help but laugh. Only a fortnight ago they started a heated conversation about the elder son, Albert, 'cos he'd been thrown out of where he was living. He's a chippie, like his dad, and got this girlfriend with her own flat, he does it all up, fitted kitchen, fitted bedroom, the lot, then when she's got it all done for nowt she chucks him! Nice one. Alana called her a bitch and Carl made the mistake of defending her. Mistake? Cue world war three. Anyway, don't see you in the *Downsman* these days, Edith, so how you keeping?"

Edith was feeling quite worn out just listening to Felicity gabbling at high speed.

"Well, I'm sorry, but it's just not the same without Reg, you know. Going to the village pub was just so us, something precious we shared. Miss him very much."

"I can understand what you mean and of course you miss things like that, don't you? Poor Reg. Poor you. I always said to Eric what a lovely couple you were. More than could be said for

11

Carl and Alana! Anyway, must be getting on. Nice chatting Edith, take care." And she was gone with a quick wave before Edith could think of any reasonable response. Oh well, something else for the notebook.

***

Carl Merde was unintentionally and accidently cementing himself to the position of prime suspect without realising it until Sheelagh challenged him with a few quietly spoken words.

"Carl, did you murder your wife? You had good reason, it would appear." This changed his whole approach with a suddenness that took the DCI by surprise. His eyes widened and his mouth dropped open, and there was fear upon his face.

"What? What? *What?* No, of course I didn't. What makes you think that? I loved her. I've told you, she was my everything and I'd have done anything for her. I loved her and looked after her, called her my little pussy cat, and thought the world of her. Kill her? Kill my pussy cat? Of course I didn't. Haven't you anything better to do, like catching the killer so I can see them brought to justice?"

Aha, Sheelagh thought. A man with two faces. Has he just woken up to the fact he's been busy incriminating himself, I wonder? He doesn't strike me as a man of much intelligence, so let's see if we can shock some more information from him.

"You were alone with Alana. Are you seriously suggesting that a third party persuaded your wife to get out of bed and to go to the patio while you slept peacefully alongside her? How did that person get in?" At this stage Carl burst into tears, burying his face in his hands and weeping profusely. Yep, thought the DCI, the defence of the guilty!

"You don't know what you're saying," he tried to shout through his hands, "and I want my solicitor," he wailed. Gotcha, decided the Chief Inspector. Or should that be meee-*ow*! Didn't murder your little pussy cat? Yeah, right.

"Alright, let's get your solicitor sorted out …."

"I want to go home …"

"I am holding you on suspicion of murdering your wife. You'll stay here and we'll get your solicitor."

12

"You can't keep me. I'm innocent. You've tricked me. Take me home."

"Just explained. You're going nowhere. Now, who's your solicitor?"

***

"Well, I always said 'Merd' as I never knew it had a silent 'e' at the end. Not that it would've made any difference, being silent, but I did wonder if it was of French origin, perhaps something unpleasant the Normans brought over with them, you know, after the conquest." Grace Cathcart was in full swing, regaling Edith with a host of data and guesswork, most of which was as pointless as it was boring. Edith listened politely and hoped it was all she needed to do.

"I heard him outside, Edith. Oh, filthy language. He was calling out to his son who was a few yards ahead of him as the family came up the street. Why people have to shout, well, I don't know, but to use offensive words, well, what's the world coming to, that's what I have to ask. Anyway Edith, my reason for calling on you is this. Back in April, for my birthday, my daughter gave me a gift voucher for afternoon tea at the Chilston Park hotel, you know, *the* Chilston Park hotel, and it's for two people. Would you like to come? Gail said it's for me and a friend, not for family use! So, please, would you like to?"

"Grace, that's so very kind, and yes, I'd love to."

"Oh that's lovely, Edith. Now when shall we go?" The two discussed dates and preferred times and Grace made the booking there and then before departing for home, leaving Edith slightly bewildered by the encounter. Nonetheless, she made a few more notes in the book.

Chapter Four

Detective Sergeant Willie Broughton was studying the notes over a warm and tasteless cup of coffee from the machine. Opposite him DS Lucy Panshaw was doing the same but without the coffee accompaniment.

He was firstly considering the neighbours either side of the murder scene. There was the couple the Merdes fell out with, Wally and Beryl Prior. They had described the Merdes as obnoxious, vulgar and offensive. According to Beryl when the Merde family gathered in the back garden it was always rather raucous with a substantial injection of bad language, despite young children being sometimes present. Wally explained that Mr & Mrs Merde liked to dominate everything, and could talk for England. But they wanted to be top dogs, and didn't like it when Mr and Mrs Prior refused to be dominated. Carl in particular liked the sound of his own voice and knew all there was to know about everything, and plainly objected when being corrected.

They knew everything about the country and managed to demonstrate they knew so little. Wally had given Willie an example. Apparently he saw Carl digging furiously at the foot of a downpipe and enquired of his neighbour what he was doing.

"I don't know Wally. Bloody drains. Jet-cleaned the drive and tried to brush all the water away into the drain but the bloody drain's blocked and all the water went in my garage! Not a surprise, is it, when the drain's stuffed full of bricks."

"You haven't got a surface drain there Carl. It's a downpipe for the gutter and that's all. There's no surface drain and the bricks are supposed to be there. It's a soakaway."

Willie chuckled out loud and Lucy looked up.

"Just reading about Carl and his soakaway. Don't you just love it when know-alls get their come-uppence? Carl took offence because Wally was right and he didn't like it. The relationship appears to have gone downhill from there! Let's look at the other neighbours."

14

"You know Willie, the more I read the more I'm convinced we might find others with a motive for murder!" He smiled in response and returned to the document in front of him. Robert and Christine Sonnel, Oak View. Also retired, like most residents of Little Scampering it seemed, they had admitted they were only on sort-of nodding terms with the Merdes, having not really taken to them believing them to be coarse Londoners. The Sonnels had moved from Canterbury where presumably, Willie mused while sporting a wicked grin, they had not been subjected to any sort of coarseness.

"How are we finding it all Lucy? I think we're looking at a mix of mainly retired people, one or two from London, others from places like the Medway towns, Maidstone, Sittingbourne, and just one or two from the country. Mrs Cathcart is the only one I can find who has lived there all her life, and Mrs Footlong who was born and bred there but moved away, and back upon retirement. Working people are a bit thin on the ground. There's the couple that run the pub, plus a young woman, Francesca Towford, who works part-time at a supermarket yet can afford a medium sized detached cottage in the country. Interesting that. But none of our business. There's a local farm worker and his wife and two teenage kids, she was born in the village, that's the connection. Then we have a dentist and her husband, he's some kind of marketing consultant, and finally a train driver and his non-working wife. No kids."

"That's seven in paid employment, Willie, bearing in mind the Trumplings actually work in the village. None of it's relevant, really, is it? Mrs Trumpling told us the Merdes used to argue in the bar, quite openly. I think she's a bit given to gossiping, but maybe you need that to be a publican in a village! Tell you what I think, Willie, almost everyone we've spoken to has been only too willing to open up to us and most of what we've obtained is pure gossip, very little of anything substantial. Local regulars at the pub back up Mrs Trumpling's account of rows between the Merdes. In short, I think Carl Merde's done up like a kipper for this one, don't you agree?"

Willie stared, eyes wide, his face a picture of astonishment.

"Done up like a kipper? Blimey, that's an old expression for one so young …. like." Lucy could detect the intended humour and elected to giggle in a silly fashion for Willie's enjoyment, even though she didn't appreciate the sarcasm. Let him have his masculine pleasure.

"My great aunt Clara used to say that. Among many other daft things. *Like*." And she poked her tongue out. "If you asked her the time she'd say – 'must be, look how dark it's getting' – she had a wealth of sayings and I loved her for it. She made it to ninety-seven; wish she'd made it to a hundred ….." And thoughts of great aunt Clara swamped her mind as she vanished into a reverie that left Willie open-mouthed.

***

Francesca Towford had been as shocked as anyone in this otherwise peaceful village, to the point of having to phone in sick unable to face work in the distressing circumstances. She'd had to cancel two appointments into the bargain, but today she'd pulled herself together anxious to avoid getting the wrong reputation and was ready for the next appointment as she climbed into her gleaming blue BMW. The police officers were not the only ones to ponder how a part-time supermarket employee could afford not just her home but her car too.

She'd kept herself to herself since moving in five years ago but always had a smile and a pleasant 'hello' for other villagers, sometimes stopping for a chat. She had, in passing, explained all too briefly that a wealthy aunt had left her a decent bequest which had enabled her to buy her own home, away from mum and dad she said, and her dream car. Telling Mrs Cathcart about her situation was as good as selling her story to a paper, for Mrs Cathcart helped spread the tale far and wide, rather as Francesca had hoped. Perhaps that tidbit would stop any further enquiries being made of her or about her.

Grace guessed, with some accuracy it must be said, that the girl was in her mid-thirties. Her good looks and remarkable figure were all too obvious, and were often noticed by various admiring males living in the village, not that she was concerned in any way. Grace also discovered that she had moved there from Tenterden, but that was where the information ran out, Francesca clearly unwilling to divulge anything further. There didn't appear to be a man in her life, or at least none that ever called at her house.

Mrs Trumpling, ever willing to gossip, surmised that she might be a 'lady of the night' to use a colloquialism, but there was no evidence to support such an opinion.

Carl Merde? Francesca considered him a nuisance. Thank God the police were going to charge him. Another problem out of the way.

***

Harry Thrack, who worked at a nearby farm, was relaxing with his wife Lizzie, while his teenage daughter tackled her school work with great attention to detail, shut away in her bedroom, isolated from the family. She wanted to go to university to study archaeology and was determined to do as well as she needed to do in her A levels a year hence. Her brother wanted to be a lorry driver, much to the chagrin of his mother, although Harry thought he should be free to do as he wished.

"So he finally killed her, did he?" he pronounced with a degree of finality that would brook no argument. "According to Felicity up the pub they was always rowing so maybe he'd had enough. Police not looking for anyone else, I'm told."

"Well Harry, there's lots we don't know yet. After all, she treated you like, well, like manure and you said, jokingly I hope, you could cheerfully strangle her. So p'raps you did her in." Harry roared with laughter which his wife joined in. They were a happy couple, by and large.

"Oh Lizzie, no I couldn't do it, but someone has. That Carl, it's him, you wait and see."

***

DCI Sheelagh Mehedren had the brothers Albert and Stephen Merde to deal with. Both were aggressive when they found dad was being held on suspicion of murder. Albert was all mouth, Stephen quieter by comparison, but it was now necessary to interview both. Sheelagh decided to go with Stephen as she reasoned he might be more emotional and revealing. Willie was

17

assigned to motor-mouth Albert and Willie decided that the privileges of rank were something he deserved to relish as soon as he could achieve his desired promotion.

In truth, interviewing Albert was simple. All Willie had to do was listen, and, when the rare opportunity presented itself, ask a pertinent question. Albert was, like his father, a self-employed chippie and was currently living with a woman near Shooters Hill in south-east London, the woman having her own small flat. The elder son proclaimed his father's innocence stressing what a loving couple mum and dad were. He went on to explain that of course they had rows, what couple didn't? Unable to stop himself in mid flow he revealed they often argued themselves to a standstill with the result they didn't speak to each other for two or three days.

Willie sat back, arms folded across his chest, a look of contempt adorning his face, as Albert let it all tumble out. What had started as a defence of his father quickly took the form of a horrible description of married life, at least as shared by Carl and Alana. Blazing rows, threats, silences, all were there. Albert thought he was protecting his dad whereas he was rather condemning him. Willie lapped it all up, actually pleased now that he'd been given this assignment.

Sheelagh was enjoying her encounter with Stephen. Tearful, sad, grieving, the young man poured out his whole life story, about his love for his mother and, interestingly, his resentment for his father. He was a 'mummy's boy' in her opinion, even to the point that he could believe the impossible, that 'daddy' had killed 'mummy'.

This was all music to her ears. Further confirmation that she had the right man. Did they need to look any further? Must keep an open mind, she reasoned, but her conviction was now firmly rooted and would not be easily disturbed. Carl Merde was the killer.

***

Edith had been busy. She'd never really paid much attention to the make up of the village and the diversity of people living there. She sat at the kitchen table with a large sheet of paper in

18

front of her on which she had drawn a rough map of the lane, and was now adding little square boxes to indicate the properties. One of these boxes was divided into five. These were the former farm workers cottages and they had been much sought after by those abandoning town life.

She wasn't quite sure why she was doing this but, having taken an interest in the Merdes, her natural curiosity had sent her in search of more detailed knowledge about where she was born and where she now lived. There were thirty two properties and four more beyond the village itself but within touching distance, these including the farm that tended to the immediate surroundings. That was where Harry Thrack worked. She found she could identify five homes where there was a lifetime connection to Little Scampering, but otherwise everyone else must've moved here.

Grace Cathcart. She'd take her map to Grace and try and piece it all together, for surely Grace must know having been born here and lived her for all of her eighty-one years. Why did villagers move away? Which incomers had been here the longest? And so on. It was all becoming rather fascinating and Edith's mind was geared-up for exploration, discovery and analysis, especially now she was retired.

***

In time the road re-opened (although the Merdes house remained sealed-off with a uniformed officer on guard outside) and villagers from all parts started to mingle for conversation, this conversation being primarily about the murder of course. Much to the joy of the Trumplings the *Downsman* was pretty busy, and drink and gossip were dispensed in equal measures as locals met there to slake their thirsts in the barmy summer weather and to discuss the dreadful event that had taken place in their midst. Felicity was orchestrating a great deal of debate and encouraging the view that Carl was guilty, whilst making sure their customers quaffed as much as possible, an art she had perfected, having a radar eye for an empty or nearly empty glass.

She could also digest many pieces of information and serve them up in whatever format suited her. Thus it was that she

19

started the rumour that there had been a fierce fight in which either Merde might've died, following the mother of all arguments in which they bellowed at each other for almost an hour. Various parts of this nonsense had been suggested by different drinkers and the whole thing was remixed as a complete story with the emphasis on it being the likely truth.

The tale ignored the fact that the neighbours might've been disturbed by the noise of a row lasting the best part of an hour, especially if it was followed by a fight. The Merdes were also unlikely to do battle without shouting!

In an otherwise quiet village overnight noise carried easily. Meanwhile the police had been analysing matters in a much more professional way, and doing so in possession of knowledge and facts denied the villagers.

Chapter Five

Sheelagh had organised a team meeting.

"Right, listen up, peoples. Pending further enquiries Carl has been released and has returned home with his sons and, of course, a police escort. The main thing at this stage is to learn if anything's missing, and his task is to check and advise us. We don't think robbery was involved but we need it confirmed. A complete blank on forensics which also points us in Carl's direction. The side gate was unbolted, no prints or anything, otherwise someone could've climbed over the rear fence from the field beyond. However, no footprints anywhere. It seems improbable that a third party managed to entice Alana out of bed without her husband's knowledge, unless, perhaps she went to investigate a noise out the back or something.

"It's all an unknown quantity. But we have to ask if there's a significance in the way she was left. Spreadeagled on her back, arms out wide, legs well apart. The post-mortem will tell us if anything else was amiss, if you get my drift. One curious thing: her face looked so normal, yes, well-wrinkled, but not registering surprise or pain or shock. She looked so calm as you can see from these photos." She pointed at the wallboard where many pictures were hung.

"We're not telling the media about the way she was left. Keep it that way. Don't mention it to anyone.

"We've learned that they weren't liked in the village, insofar as nobody seems to have a good word to say about the Merdes, although some people have clearly drawn on hearsay rather than made their own minds up. I am taking to the concept of Alana being the intended victim, largely because of the way she was left, which might rule out robbery as an initial motive. I think this was pre-meditated murder, pure and simple, and Mr Merde is in my sights.

"They loved to lie out on the patio in the warm weather, so did he decide that was where she had to meet her end? It does appear that certain persons disliked her intensely and with good reason, but enough to kill her? Keep an open mind, guys, cos you never know. This enquiry ain't finished yet. Any questions?"

There were a number of queries for the DCI to deal with, but then it was time to get back on track.

***

Edith couldn't believe her luck. Grace proved very enthusiastic about her new project, people-mapping the village, and joined in with great passion and fervour.

"Is this to do with the murder?" Grace had asked.

"Well, it wasn't actually, but I suppose the murder prompted it, because I realised how little I knew about all my neighbours, not that I'm nosey or anything," she added quickly, "but I do think it's nice to get a better picture of today's Little Scampering and how its changed over the years."

"But it could be useful, especially if Mr Merde isn't the killer."

"I'm not sure how Grace, and everyone is sure he killed his wife, so I'm certain the police think so too."

"Yes, but nothing is certain yet, is it? After all Edith, he's been released, hasn't he, and I'm not sure we'd want the police to put a madman back in our midst. So suppose it was someone else?"

The idea was not new to Edith but she was surprised her friend had thought along those lines when everyone she'd met had roundly condemned Carl Merde to the metaphorical gallows. Yes, it was an interesting thought although how her own investigation could be of value in nailing the guilty party escaped her.

***

Peter Digbin looked at his wife, cowering in the corner, clutching her left arm where he'd hit her with all his might before throwing her to the floor.

"Just do as you're told, right? Don't argue with me or you'll finish up like that Merde woman. You look after my home, right? You're a housewife, you do the cooking, cleaning, washing and cater for my every need. You were supposed to give me children

22

but that's gone out the window. We can be a loving couple, you and me, and I don't have to punish you. I can be kind to you all the time as long as you don't forget your place. So no, you can't find a part-time job. By now you should be looking after our kids, that was the arrangement, but you can't have kids can you? Only found out *after* we were wed. Gawd. Now, I look after you Alison, don't I? My money's good and we live well, and I take care of you. Just behave, that's all I ask of you. Now make me a cuppa, and don't forget I'm on duty early tomorrow. Need a good night's sleep, can't be driving a train half-asleep, can I?"

***

Sheena Bargeman completed her crossword and sighed. Her husband, Trevor, was away on a project at the moment, staying in Alnmouth, Northumberland, and he'd missed all the excitement of the murder. He had offered to come straight home but she'd turned him down saying that she wasn't really troubled, was perfectly alright, and his work was more important.

It had been a tough day at the dental practice where too many people for her liking, patients and staff alike, knew where she lived and wanted to know 'all about it' when there was so little to tell. At least the patients were restricted when it came to conversation once their mouths were wide open!

Her thoughts had more than once turned to Carl Merde. When the Merdes arrived Carl had advertised the fact he was a retired carpenter and she and Trevor had engaged him to fit some cupboards in the bedroom. The task had clearly been beyond him and he'd had to send for his son, Albert, to rescue him. At least Albert did a good job. Both of them could talk the talk, and Carl had a wealth of excuses, blaming everyone and everything but himself while making a complete bodge of the job.

Since then they had discreetly warned close friends and neighbours, and, as far as they knew, Carl had not worked again in the village. But Alana did have an altercation with Trevor when she realised that the Bargemans had been spreading the ill-word. Sheena didn't witness it, but Trevor complained she was certainly foul-mouthed and very threatening, not how he expected a lady to behave.

23

"She'll get her day of reckoning," he'd agreed with Sheena, and now that day had dawned.

***

Grace was proving to be a positive mine of information. And there was a bonus. She'd kept a diary since she was thirteen years of age and, sure enough, comings and goings in the village, as well as any other notable events, were duly recorded. By this medium Edith found the exact date she left Little Scampering and the precise date of her return, Grace adding a footnote 'welcome home Edith' under her entry. A heart-warming addition for Edith.

Of course, there was an entry for the day the Merdes arrived. They'd bought the house previously owned by Hugh and Constance Ambledown who, as old age approached in a rush, had gone to a modest bungalow in Sittingbourne to be nearer to their daughter, Marion, and to enjoy life on one level. They loved their garden but it was getting beyond them and their bungalow had a much smaller plot they could keep on top of. Just the ticket!

With meticulous care Grace turned the pages from that day forward, hoping to find references to the Merdes. There was a note that Sheena Bargeman was quietly advising people not to use Carl as a carpenter as he was 'nothing but a jobbing chippie, work of class being outside his capabilities'. She paused suddenly on another matter. She'd noted that Alison Digbin was sporting a black eye a week after appearing with a split lip and Grace was concerned that her husband had hit her. Not that she could interfere or do anything about it, but she'd written that if it was true then Mr Digbin was not a gentleman and was as evil as could be.

But then they came upon it. Grace sat up straight and gasped. A week after the black eye incident she'd written that she saw Carl Merde leaving Alison's house during the day, and she knew Peter was at work. A week later and Grace had seen it again, but had assumed the Digbins were foolishly using his services as a carpenter. Two days after that she bumped into Alison, so she wrote, and asked her outright, noting the woman blushed to the roots and stuttered, finally saying that they had considered asking

24

him to do something relatively simple but had decided against it. 'I think she's not being truthful' was the note appended.

"My, my, Grace. Nobody could possibly get away with anything while you've been living here! You really have kept a record, haven't you. Do you think Carl was seeing Alison behind Peter's back?"

"Possibly. Must've thought so at the time. If she has a nasty, controlling husband, the sort you read about, and he hits her, perhaps she found some respite in the arms of another."

"Carl Merde doesn't sound like anyone's idea of a paramour! But I must say I'm impressed with your diaries. And you've kept them all, right from when you were thirteen?"

"I have, Edith, every one. And now they could be coming in useful."

Chapter Six

Willie Broughton had been seeing much of Sian Stramer. At first he'd thought her to be all-body and no mind, the reaction of a typical male when confronted by a tall, long-legged, attractive but aloof woman. But when they were working on the murder of Gareth Modlum, also out in the Kent countryside, they found some common ground and went on a date. Still emotionally shocked by events, notably Molly Penderman's close call with death, they simply sat and talked and Willie learned that there was much more to Sian than he'd realised. She was a deep thinker, opinionated, sharp-witted and good company.

Now their dates were more meaningful giving both considerable pleasure. Whether the relationship would develop was in the lap of the gods, but for now it spelled happiness.

There was not a lot of happiness being shared around amongst officers working on Alana Merde's case. DS Lucy Panshaw was convinced of Carl's guilt whereas Willie did not share the same commitment. The DCI would need an awful lot of persuading but was at least prepared to explore every possible avenue despite most being dead ends. Sian said they should be giving more attention to the position the body was laid out in as she felt it was a clue in itself.

"Could be symbolic," she commented, "but I reckon it was somebody making a statement about Alana herself. Have we checked on the marital relationship?" Sheelagh shook her head once. "We've been told they rowed a lot, sometimes quite publicly, but some people are like that. It doesn't mean anything, just their way of living. I'd find it hurtful, y'know, having an argument with a loved one, but I've met people who don't give a damn. A row is part of conversation and it doesn't hurt their feelings. Sounds horrible. But there you go. And another thing. If it wasn't Carl then perhaps it was someone getting back at him. You know, kill his wife, not the person he or she had a dispute with."

"Good point, Sian," Sheelagh agreed, nodding her head and looking around as if to say 'and I'm surprised nobody else thought of that' before rising slowly from her chair. "Needless to say if we haven't got our man there's a killer out there. Willie, Lucy, you've studied the statements from the villagers, anything in there need more investigation?"

"Don't like to suggest this, ma'am, but I think we ought to interview them all again." Willie saw the look of annoyance in the DCI's face but pressed on. "Know it means time, but I reckon they might cough up a bit more if they think we're investigating new leads, and it would give us the chance to ask more pertinent questions of some of 'em." Lucy saw Sheelagh's expression and ploughed straight in.

"Ma'am, I think Willie's right. There are things I'd like to ask some of the villagers relevant to their statements now we've got ideas, and it might work if they think we're not convinced about Carl. Could even put the wind up some of them! You know, murderer on the loose in the village."

Willie and Lucy stood close together wearing expressions that suggested they might be waiting to have their ears metaphorically boxed. Sheelagh didn't disappoint.

"Right. My underlings want me to waste precious resources on a wild goose chase at a time when we are desperately pleading for more funding, and an ever-watchful long-suffering taxpayer is keeping us under constant surveillance for signs of pointless expenditure." There was a brief silence. Suddenly Sheelagh's face erupted with a fierce grin. "Okay, we'll do it." Sighs of relief all round. "Since you two clever-clogs have outwitted your supreme leader once again the pair of you can organise this. And if it goes tits-up it'll be spankings all round." A mild giggle escaped amongst those present and ran around the room.

"Back to work, children," Sheelagh bellowed as she headed for her office.

***

Thanks to Grace's diaries a picture of the occupation of Little Scampering down the recent ages was emerging. In the post-war years it was a close-knit community as you might find anywhere in the country, but gradually employment opportunities decreased and that was when born-and-bred villagers started

27

moving away. Most inhabitants today were retired and most had moved there from urban areas, the more recent arrivals tending to be the ones with plenty of money. This was part of the reason property prices were high which in turn also forced younger people who had grown up in family homes here to move out. But then the young nowadays tended to prefer the bright lights of town to the comparative peace and remoteness of the countryside.

Grace and Edith reminisced about the village shop which had died a long time ago. It had also been the post office but that convenience had vanished long before the place closed for good.

"Mrs Bradshaw had time for everyone," Edith recalled from her earlier life, "and always stocked plenty of sweets for the children."

"Yes," Grace added, taking up the story, "and when she left a lovely couple, Mr and Mrs Burgan, took over and she ensured they stocked all kinds of wool, so handy for those of us who liked knitting. Our little shops are lost forever, Edith, and we've lost something precious if you ask me."

"What happened when the Burgans closed down, Grace?"

"The premises was bought by a couple from Rainham and completely renovated and converted. Cost them a pretty penny but then they had money to burn in those days. Not so now. Boom and bust, my dear Edith."

"Oh Grace, do tell!"

"Well, some of it's tittle-tattle, of course. Anyway, they had it all. Flash cars, took expensive holidays, you know, Seychelles, Thailand, Bermuda, you name it, they'd been there. Used to boast about it in the pub. Boasted about how much they'd spent doing up the former stores, that kind of thing. He was something to do with money, a sort of financial adviser I'd heard, but don't quote me on that. She'd stayed at home to raise the children, who'd left before they moved here.

Not worked since, so I believe, but no need by all accounts.

"Retirement came and you might've believed they'd be set up for life. But over time things went quiet, that is, they stopped going to the pub, sold their two big cars and bought a smaller second-hand one. I wondered if one of them was ill. I did ask her but she thanked me for being so concerned, and reassured me

28

they were both fighting fit. The holidays dried up. They hardly ever go away these days, so I reckon some financial catastrophe overtook them. Perhaps an unwise investment? Well, anyway, it also became clear that Falconwood Cottage, as they called it, was starting to fall into disrepair.

"I don't know this for a fact, but I think they may have contacted Mr Merde when they heard he was a retired carpenter, but I have no idea if they used him. Probably not. His reputation may have preceded him by then! Oh, and they're not married, you know."

"No, I didn't know. Thought they were Mr and Mrs Parkforth ....."

"Oh no my dear. I think that was the kind of respectable front they wanted to adopt but in a small place like this the truth leaks out! He's Donald Parkforth and she's Belinda Thredsham."

It was time for Edith to make some more notes. Just imagine, she thought to herself, all this time I thought they were a quiet, retired married couple! Still, people don't get married much these days, she mused.

***

Kathy Pilchard stared out through the French windows at the back of her house. She was still happy enough. It was just sad that she and husband were simply good friends these days. All the life had gone out of their love and she felt horribly responsible although she knew she had no good reason to think that.

Shortly after he retired Kevin had become mixed up with that widow over the road, Nancy Harmand. Kathy was so trusting she never put two and two together until he confessed that frightful November night, forever indelibly printed in her mind. There was a real thunder storm with so much lightning and heavy claps that shook the windows. It wasn't so much a backdrop as a foredrop as Kevin's story fell before her completing an image of a Wagnerian drama as her whole life unravelled.

The best husband a woman could have, father to three beautiful girls. He'd always been there for her and the family. Utterly devoted, until Nancy got her claws into him. Kathy forgave him, anxious to save her marriage, but of course things

29

hadn't been the same since. They couldn't be. She could forgive but not forget. And she couldn't trust him again. He'd reverted to being the wonderful husband and father, but she couldn't get the matter out of her mind or her heart.

By agreement they hadn't told the children. Their offspring had all flown the nest before they moved to Little Scampering to enjoy their retirement. Better they never knew.

Right now Kathy was thinking about the murder. She was wondering if Alana had strayed and Carl had taken his revenge rather than forgive her the transgression. Or had he done it so that he could take up with another woman? Perhaps widow Harmand!

She shuddered but not from the cold. It was another very hot day. She had shocked herself by wondering, all of a sudden, if Kevin had wanted to get rid of her, and if so, by what means. Kathy pulled herself together. Thank God he wasn't like that, anymore than she was. But the scenario left a nasty taste that wouldn't go away just yet.

***

In the *Downsman* Roger Kempson was regaling a newspaper reporter with all kinds of gossip, most of it unfounded, most of it related to the Merdes. The reporter was stifling a yawn. She hadn't come here to ingest this kind of knowledge and was conscious that time was a-wasting while he prattled on and on. He inadvertently provided the solution by knocking his beer over. Sally Cainton, displaying great agility, slipped out of the way and, while Roger went for assistance she swiftly departed but only as far as the tables outside.

Here she fell in with Mr and Mrs Harper who, it turned out, rather helpfully, lived next door to the Sonnels, the neighbours of the Merdes. This was a better prospect, she realised, than simply talking to other locals. She needed to get closer to the scene of the crime, as it were.

The Harpers were reticent and unwilling to talk much about either the Sonnels or the Merdes, which made a pleasant change from the gossip-mongers Sally had encountered, but was frustrating for a hack after a story.

However, Mrs Harper let slip a rumour that Alana had been seeing another man but she had no idea who, and stressed it was merely hearsay. Sally persisted. How much of a rumour? And eventually she struck gold. Mrs Harper, having divulged the tale, was reluctant to continue, but the reporter had well-oiled persuasive powers and, with a little gentle prodding and kind words, came into possession of information denied others including the police, although she didn't know that yet.

Mrs Harper revealed that she herself had seen widower Ken Waghorn leaving the Merdes on a day when Carl Merde was away helping his son, Albert, with some work or other.

"According to one or two villagers he was often there when Carl wasn't. But he was probably just a friend. I don't want to spread gossip, Sally, and it is all hearsay, can't stress that enough. You should try the Sonnels, or the Priors, you know, the other side of the Merdes, as they may be able to help you more."

Yes, thought Sally. You've put yourself in the muck, haven't you, and now you want a get-out clause. Pass the buck, get rid of me, send me to the neighbours. And I've been to both and got short shrift. But maybe try again with this fresh information? Yes, maybe that's exactly what I'll do, ace reporter that I am!

Chapter Seven

One couple who were seemingly loved by everyone were the Nagarkas. They came from India and had trained in the medical profession here before returning briefly to their homeland for their wedding. It was an arranged marriage but it appeared to have been very successful. They came back to England to launch their careers, Deepak as a hospital doctor and his wife, Poojah as a nurse who finished her own career working in a nursing home.

They'd lived near Sittingbourne where their children had grown up and set off on their own lives. Deepak and Poojah came to Little Scampering a few years ago ready for retirement which they were now enjoying, and they were the epitome of the expression 'would do anything for anyone'.

When Grace Cathcart's car had reached the end of its life and had to be humanely put down, Deepak took her to local garages and helped her choose a suitable replacement, ensuring that she wasn't ripped off. She was thus the proud owner of a Ford Ka in which she would be taking Edith to Chilston Park for their afternoon tea treat tomorrow.

Both ladies were keenly looking forward to the occasion, but had been completely pre-occupied with Edith's map which was now almost complete. Each property was labelled with its occupiers and referenced to the data in the notebook, this information being extensive in some cases, patchy in others, and bald for one or two, there being no narrative of interest to add. Deepak Nagarka and his wife were among the last entries.

Edith had met Poojah in the street and they had discussed the horror that had befallen their village, Poojah being surprisingly sympathetic towards Carl and sorry for poor Alana.

"I am sad for him," she said, "especially if he didn't kill her because I cannot imagine the shock of finding your loved one dead. Poor Alana, and yes, I do feel sorry for Carl even if he is the murderer, because he may have been driven to desperate measures and will regret his actions until his dying day." Yes, thought Edith, a display of compassion missing in all too many folk, bearing in mind we don't know the circumstances or the truth about Carl's involvement. She continued on her way feeling a little chastened by Poojah's reaction, despite not being one to have rushed to condemn Carl.

***

Sally Cainton was made to feel most unwelcome at both the Sonnels' and the Priors' homes. Her rumour, which she tried to sell as being appreciably more than that, failed to open up the couples she was interviewing, who denied any knowledge of Ken Waghorn's visits. However, when the police called later it was a different story.

Detective Constables Sian Stramer and Hassana Achebe, who had worked together on the Gareth Modlum murder, were covering that part of the village and arrived first at the Sonnels' Oak View Cottage. Christine opened the door and was swift to mention the reporter's call, deciding she might as well tell the truth.

"Look officers, to be honest we did notice Mr Waghorn calling from time to time but thought nothing of it. One villager calling upon another. Happens all the time without anything, well, without anything *sinister* involved. But this reporter woman was trying to imply that he'd been here when Carl wasn't at home, and suggesting there might've been, well, might have been hanky-panky going on. I cannot imagine that was so, he's such a nice gentleman, Mr Waghorn."

"That's alright, Mrs Sonnel," Sian soothed, "these reporters get in our way, and they're not above making it up or embellishing a rumour to make it spicy. It's their way of searching out a story that'll sell papers. We're trying to solve a dreadful crime and we're only interested in the truth." Mr Sonnel had reached the door and had overheard some of the conversation, so asked what was going on. Sian gave him a precis.

"Oh I see," he said, "Well we were right not to tell her anything, then." Sian nodded, then spoke.

"We're grateful you could mention Mr Waghorn's visits to us. It's all just for the record at the moment and it's things like this that we need to build a composite picture of the village. What goes on here in all innocence is vital to eliminating those who were not involved that fateful night. I hope you understand." Both did, and the visit ended at that point. The next port of call, the Priors', would prove much more rewarding for Sian and Hassana.

***

Edith sat alone at her kitchen table studying her enterprise. What an undertaking it had been! Were there any clues there, she wondered? Were there any connections she couldn't see, connections that might point to a guilty party? Of course there was nothing obvious and she began to consider what a pointless exercise she'd been through.

But wait! If Carl wasn't the killer then either it was an outsider or it was a fellow villager, and if the latter then his or her name was on her plan. Who dunnit? Who indeed. She suspected that in one of those crime novels the least likely candidate would turn out to be the killer. Oh, it could be one of so many! In truth, would any villager hate them so much to commit murder? Who could possibly be so cold-blooded and ruthless? Then her thoughts turned elsewhere. Did someone have a particular reason for assassination? Was Alana, for example, about to reveal a bad secret that someone wanted kept quiet? Now there's a thought!

Or could we even be looking at a love affair gone wrong? Something along those lines maybe.

Then again, if it was an outsider the issue opens a whole can of worms that she could never hope to get to the bottom of. Better leave it to the police!

***

"Hello Mr Prior, DC Stramer and DC Achebe, sorry to trouble you again." Sian went through the details as before, asking about Ken Waghorn. Mr Prior looked directly into her eyes and appeared very resigned. There was a moment's silence.

"Do please come in. Don't think this is for the doorstep." Aha, thought Sian, that's what I wanted to hear! Mrs Prior was knitting in the lounge, a large, spacious room with the patio door wide open, and a ceiling fan twirling above. "It's the police, dear, and it's about Mr Waghorn. Must be something in what that confounded reporter was saying after all. Please sit down ladies, oh I'm sorry, should say officers these days, I suppose."

"Pleased to be called a lady Mr Prior. Thank you. No apology necessary." They all smiled, Mrs Prior stopped knitting and Sian and Hassana sat together on a three-seater settee. "Now, what did you tell the reporter?"

"Oh, oh, nothing at all. Denied it all. But it was true. Mr Waghorn was often next door, and in the absence of Mr Merde. They used to sit on the patio for a drink and then go indoors. If the weather was inclement they stayed indoors anyway. We're keen gardeners, love the outdoors, very proud of the garden, well, my wife's head-gardener," he managed a nervous giggle, "and I'm just the boy really, but we both find it our paradise. There's a six-metre fence there now, Mr Merde had it put up when they were accusing us of 'gawping' at them all the time, did you ever, but it used to be lower and we could see into their garden, just as they could see into ours. If anyone did any 'gawping' it was them."

Hassana felt quite breathless just listening to the garrulous Mr Prior, but if he was about to run out of steam there was help at hand. Mrs Prior took up the dialogue.

"Shocking couple they were. Shocking. Said such nasty things, and I really don't know why. Everything they accused us of were things they were doing to us, for example, as my husband explained, gawping. Their word. They used to stare through our net curtains to try and make out if we were looking at them. Now, if that isn't an invasion of privacy I don't know what is. One day, when they went out and saw my husband mowing in our front garden Mr Merde said loudly to his wife 'it's only Rambo pretending to mow the lawn so he can see what we're doing'. How can you pretend to mow the lawn? That's how stupid they are. Unintelligent."

"Rambo?" asked an incredulous Hassana.

"Oh, just one of his stupid nicknames, that's all. He called me a nasty old goat and an ugly old hag. If there was an ugly old hag it was his wife. A face permanently screwed up with evil. And she was evil …."

The interview lasted about another five minutes before an exhausted Sian found an excuse to abandon it. But they'd learned enough about Ken Waghorn. And they'd learned much about the Priors themselves!

***

"Hello Mr Waghorn" Lucy Panshaw called out with all the cheerfulness and bonhomie she could muster, decorating her face with a lovely disarming smile, all intended to put him at his ease. Hassana had messaged her as soon as she'd left the Priors. "Can I come in, please?"

"Well, yes, I suppose so," but he stood in the hall, closed the front door and did not advance any further into the house. He was anything but at ease.

Lucy explained in a nutshell what she'd been told and Ken Waghorn's face dropped as his eyes searched the floor, the walls, the ceiling, anywhere but the officer.

"Might've guessed you'd come. Had a reporter trying it on, but I just denied it. But I'm afraid it's true." His eyes were now glued to the floor in front of Lucy. "I'm a lonely old widower. Would love a bit of female company, but it's hard to come by. Met Mrs Merde along the lane, had a chat, and she invited me round. Told me to come the next Tuesday afternoon, I think it was, as Mr Merde would be working in London. I was reading signals that did indeed turn out to be there and I couldn't stop myself.

"Went round, had a natter and a cuppa, but we were making eyes at each other and we finished up inside having a kiss and a cuddle. Never had more than that. But she told me her husband wasn't romantic and there was no intimacy, and I dived straight in. Desperate old man." And he shook his head without removing his eyes from the carpet.

"We packed it in ages ago, because the neighbours had seen us together too much, and in a small village like this you can't scratch your ar….., sorry, can't scratch your ear without someone noticing. Not been back since. And that's over a year ago. Does Mr Merde have to know?" Only now did he look at Lucy, and with sweet, pleading eyes.

36

"Not necessarily. I hope, for your sake, he doesn't need to be told. For the present this is just for our information, Mr Waghorn." He nodded slowly and returned to studying the floor. "But we're having to make these checks to ensure that we catch the right culprit. You told us you were alone the night of the murder so nobody could verify that, I suppose." He looked up again.

"No. Nobody. Lonely old widower, me. Just like I told you."

Chapter Eight

The post-mortem established the knife went straight through Alana's heart, there were no other injuries or signs of violence, and there had been no sexual interference. Death almost instantaneous. The police had not made public the fact that her corpse had been neatly arranged in a spreadeagled fashion and it was quite clear to them that the killer had organised the body thus. It also ruled out suicide; difficult once you're dead to tidy things up! Had Alana been left like that to spite Carl who was bound to find her? Had Carl, if he was the murderer, left her arranged in that way as a kind of revenge for some perceived crime against him? Questions, questions.

Willy and Lucy were pleased with themselves, for their suggestion was bearing fruit. Talking to the residents again was proving beneficial and Sheelagh Mehedren did not like it one bit. This was, in part, because she could see no other culprit but Carl, and these diversions were all based on hearsay, in some cases quite possibly a retaliation against a couple who had upset people.

Grace Cathcart had, this time around, mentioned the business about Alison Digbin who had been questioned again, denied it all as nonsense, the work of a nosey neighbour, and had therefore suffered another beating at Peter's hands once the police had departed. She swore to her husband Carl had never been there, but he dealt out his own form of justice anyway, as a warning. Grace would've been heartbroken and horrified to learn that her information, most definitely not gossip, had led to such fearsome retribution.

To the DCI having non-suspect suspects created red-herrings they could do without. Nobody had a motive that might've driven them to kill, now did they? But Willie and Lucy were fired up and it was time to throw a bucket of cold water over them.

She might also have considered throwing said bucket of cold water over Edith and Grace had she known what they were up to.

***

38

Being a little early for their booking Edith and Grace wandered around the parkland surrounding the Chilston Park hotel, admiring the lake and more especially the elegant architecture of the main building. Both had looked into its history and found it fascinating. There was a slight wooshing sound that caught their attention and away in the distance they could see the top of a high-speed train heading eastwards towards Ashford.

"Southeastern," announced Grace, knowledgeably, "not Eurostar."

"I'm impressed," replied an impressed Edith, "how do you tell the difference?"

"Southeastern are deep blue, Eurostar much lighter."

"How on earth do you know all this?"

"I know you will think me odd, my dear, but I'm a bit of a train fanatic at heart. And yes, I adore the steam engines of old." Edith didn't think her odd at all, but was quite amazed that her friend had such a pastime. "Yes, I suppose you could say I have a wide range of interests, hobbies I imagine you'd call them, and our current project is right up my street, literally. Our village is proving rather more diverse than we realise, wouldn't you agree?"

"Yes, most definitely Grace. And it's a bit unsettling, if you ask me. We're uncovering a number of people who might have committed the murder! Seriously, if it's not Carl then it could actually be one of our own suspects."

"Precisely, and that adds to the fun, eh?" Both ladies smiled, checked their watches, and made their way at a casual stroll towards Reception.

***

"Okay Willie, hit me." Willie gave his boss a sideways look of mock concern and added a wry grin to his countenance.

"Funny expression that, ma'am. Wouldn't want to actually hit you."

"Listen, my boy, if you did you would be writhing in all kinds of agony, and some injuries you might not recover from."

"That's brought tears to my eyes, ma'am."

39

"Yay, and so would my attack." The two officers shared a strong bond, a good working relationship that enabled them to step outside normal boundaries, each knowing how far they could go.

"Right." Willie took up the briefing. "Carl's in the frame. Nobody else gets close. It was an old carving knife, a bit rusty near the handle ...."

"That's bad," Sheelagh interrupted, "fancy using that. A bit rusty, might've caused an infection!"

They both chuckled. It was their way, their humour and it helped them through the worst aspects of a case like this without them becoming emotionally involved.

"Any...way ....." Willie continued, his pronunciation and pause almost sounding insubordinate, "they reckon it had traces of soil on it, not local soil, so can't tie it to Little Scampering. We understand nothing's missing from the Merdes house, so that might rule out burglary, theft, whatever. The significance of Alana's position: spreadeagle. Our experts say it could be something sexual, it could be spiritual, could be symbolic as in a bird soaring free in the sky, or as in a bird of prey ...."

"Yes, I like that," Sheelagh interrupted again, "the idea of her being a bird of prey, swooping on her victims like neighbours or lovers and so on. Sorry Willie, please continue."

"If only I was given the chance ...."

"Watch it, mate, you're talking to real bird of prey here!"

"It has been suggested it might be religious. In churches the lectern is often in the shape of an eagle with the bible on its back. One theory is that it represents the Word of God being carried far and wide by the bird."

"Okay, so are we reading too much in to this? In her tiny little nightdress thingy perhaps the killer was just saying she was cheap and anyone's. Carl might have thought that, especially if he knew or had guessed about Ken."

"Same could apply to Ken himself, if he was the killer."

"Good point, Willie. But by the same token we could say that of anyone wanting to make that point including half of Little Scampering it would seem. Sorry Willie, but I think we're getting carried away here. None of these people had enough dislike or even hatred to kill, and in that cold-blooded manner, surely?"

"I know it looks that way ma'am, but victims have been slaughtered for less." Sheelagh nodded, knowing it was much the truth.

***

Stephen Merde was beside himself with grief. His mother brutally slain. And to make it worse the police felt that his father might be the one with metaphorical blood on his hands. In such a state it was but a short journey to start hating Carl, and with resentment and bitterness building within, Stephen was beginning to wish his father dead.

Albert was also grief-stricken but refused to accept that his dad had anything to do with it. Thus was brother set against brother. Stephen's wife Zoe had come down for a day, could see this rift developing, and tried to step in to mediate which only made matters worse. Finally that day it almost came to blows.

"Our beloved mother called Zoe a bitch with good reason, as you well know Steve ...."

"She called *all* your girlfriends bitches, and they were. You've got four kids by three different women, at least me and Zoe are married and our daughter's ours. Your latest bitch has a daughter by someone else ...."

"Look," cried an exasperated and offended Zoe, "that's enough. For God's sake, stop it. Have neither of you any respect for your mother's memory? For pities sake, stop this now." This produced in lull in hostilities but she didn't doubt they would start afresh once she'd gone.

***

"In those TV police dramas it's usually the least likely one who commits the crime and it sometimes takes several episodes to sort it out," Grace remarked as she helped herself to a salmon sandwich. The ladies had been shown to their seats, the tray of goodies had arrived, three tiers of it, and the teapot had just been added to the table. "These are very comfortable armchairs, aren't they Edith?"

41

Edith took an egg sandwich, eyeing up the scones which were still warm

"Oh very comfortable, and this is so very kind of you Grace, it really is. Yes, I thought the same thing myself, but who is the least likely apart from us of course?" Grace giggled politely.

"Stabbed to death, poor woman. Now here is a terrible thought. We have a doctor and a nurse in the village. Surely they would know where to stab a person."

"Oh Grace, what a shocking thing to say. You really are naughty." They laughed heartily and both reached for another sandwich. "For that matter we have a dentist and you might say the same about her." Grace rocked with gentle laughter.

"Dear me, Edith, dentists don't know how to kill, they just know exactly how to cause extreme pain!" Their laughter was causing other customers to glance in their direction and they realised they needed to tone it down. Not the place for such a raucous demonstration of mirth. Happily it was time to move on to the scones, cream and jam, and they were absolutely delicious, as was the freshly brewed tea.

"So tell me, Grace, where does that leave us?"

"I think in all seriousness that any number of our fellow villagers disliked one or other or both, but I am curious about Carl and what he was getting up to, and then there's the business about Mr Waghorn that reporter mentioned. I don't think it's cut and dried, Edith. I'm asking myself if there's an unknown quantity here, to use an expression." She paused and bit into a scone, chewed it, allowed it to put a smile of satisfaction on her face, and then continued.

"Mmmm ….. delicious. Well, Edith, is there more to a situation than we know about? That's what I mean. We know about Mr Waghorn now, for example, but supposing there was something very unsavoury about his involvement with Alana, perhaps something criminal?" Having finished her two scones Edith was perusing the cakes on the top tier and chose a splendid looking item, placing it on her plate, before answering.

"A good point Grace. I hadn't thought of that. But Carl strikes me as being more of the criminal type than Alana."

"I agree on the face of it, Edith, but then you never really know people, do you? Alana could turn out to be a criminal mastermind, perhaps taken out by the Eltham mafia." Edith spluttered into the cup she was taking a sip from, looked at her friend who was sporting a wicked grin, and realised it had been said in jest.

But had it?

***

Sally Cainton pulled a range of faces as she studied the list of villagers she'd spoken to. One thing struck her, one potentially important thing.

That Mrs Footlong and Mrs Cathcart: got the distinct feeling they knew more than they were saying, she reasoned with herself. I'd go so far as to say they were hiding something. I've got a reporter's nose for this, and I've got a reporter's inquisitive mind, and I've got a reporter's shark-like teeth when I want to sink them into something. Time to exercise my not unimpressive skills on these ladies. They won't outwit me. It's time to cough to aunt Sally my darlings.

Chapter Nine

The duty solicitor had made it plain. Carl Merde was in serious trouble and instructed not to speak to the media. He was lucky not to be in custody. In fact he was mostly sitting quietly at home, unable to visit the patio, that was too painful, and generally doing very little other than staring into space. There were no tears. He didn't read the papers, watch television, listen to the radio, and was eating hardly anything.

Albert, being self-employed, had to get back to work, but Stephen was alright for a couple of days more thanks to sympathetic employers. Although he didn't say anything to his father he was increasingly convinced of his dad's guilt, and his contempt, anger and bitterness was manifest in everything he did for Carl.

"I didn't do it, Steve," Carl suddenly announced one morning. "I loved your mum, would've done anything for her, and I've lost her, and I can't stand the pain. Just believe me, Steve. I know you think I did it. Albert hasn't said a word, it's that I can pick it up from the way you're treating me, and I want you to know I'm innocent."

"I loved mum too," Stephen wailed. "Somebody killer her, right here, right outside on the patio while you slept in your bed, and I hate you for that. And if you are charged and convicted you cannot begin to imagine what sort of person that hatred will make me." Now, for the first time in days, tears trickled down Carl's face as he sat, head bowed, his arms in his lap.

"I didn't do it, Steve, I didn't do it," he sobbed quietly, "and I had no idea she'd got out of bed and gone to the patio. We're an old couple son, we get up the night, y'know, go to the toilet or we just can't sleep, it's what happens when you get old, and we don't always know when the other one has got up. For God's sake, Steve, don't hate me for that."

But without a word Stephen left the room. He was full of tears but didn't want his father to see him crying and he didn't want his father to think the situation had changed between them.

***

"I do not like it, I do not like it one little bit," Sally Cainton said aloud to herself while her facial expression suggested she liked it very much.

"A village full of widows, okay, slight exaggeration, and lonely Ken Waghorn has to go after forbidden fruit. Why? The thrill of the chase? The thrill of doing something naughty in his old age?

Or maybe Alana was desperate, who knows? But whatever, it's worth a bit more digging, because I sense a real story coming out of this. Hold on, hold on. Perhaps he *did* try his luck with other ladies, a success here and there, occasional rejection. Kenny baby, you're beginning to look like a bit of a lad! I wonder. I wonder if its worth my while dressing appropriately and flirting with him. I'll soon get a good idea cos I'm good with body language and all that, and I'm ruthless!

"Dear Mr Waghorn … mmm … interesting name that …. I'm a-coming for you."

***

Francesca Towford returned home from the supermarket, changed out of her uniform, showered and relaxed in a towelling robe. Phew, its hot, she thought, and settled for an ice-cold glass of water from the fridge rather than the glass of ice-cold wine she really fancied. I've still got some driving to do and mustn't turn up smelling of alcohol. She stood and went to the bedroom and the chest of drawers where she selected a bra that always brought out the best in the features it held, and a pair of black and red knickers. Don't like the colours myself, not really feminine, but they seem to turn men on.

Funny creatures, men, she concluded, but so predictable. Makes the job that much easier, I suppose, and with that threw herself on the bed and cuddled a pillow. Within the hour, and after a light lunch, she was on the road again and bound for Tenterden. Thank God for air-conditioning. It made journeys bearable in this awful heat, and I can arrive fresh as a daisy, that's what my mum used to say. Fresh as a daisy.

45

As she drove she thought about that wretched reporter, nosey cow. Trying to get me to talk about other people, trying to entice me into saying things I'd rather not. Trouble is, I expect she's succeeding with others and has no doubt heard all the rumours about me. Oh well, so what if its true? I'm only defrauding the taxman, and isn't that everyone's duty?

She sniggered at the thought. Wonder what my mum, gawd rest her soul, would say about my little side-line? And she laughed out loud.

***

Katie Marchant had prepared one of her tasty curries to share with her partner, Sheelagh Mehedren. They lived together on Sheppey and as they both more or less worked shifts the time they spent in each other's company was precious, and this evening was to be one of them. They'd met many years ago when the bus Katie was driving stopped for an accident that happened right in front of her. In a more junior capacity than now Sheelagh was one of the officers sent to the incident and she provided just the level of comfort a shocked Katie needed, adding more comfort later that evening when she called upon the bus driver.

Nowadays she drove for Chalkwell who had taken over the island's bus services and always seemed quite content with her lot. After all, there was Sheelagh to look forward to.

After their splendid meal, washed down with a particularly notable Frascati, they were relaxing on the sofa and chattering about their respective days.

"Know you can't talk about cases in detail, Shee, but how's things going with that Little Scampering murder? See online they reckon the husband's killed her."

"I know, and I wish they wouldn't speculate like that. Just twixt you and me, Kats, its all purely circumstantial. Keep that under your hat."

"Sure, sure. And Willie Broughton, is he on the case?"

"Yes, and I wouldn't tell him this, but I couldn't do without him, he's ace. And he's willing to learn from me and there's not many blokes would admit that! Bit disturbed about one development though. He's seeing Sian Stramer, one of my DCs, and I don't like colleagues mixing like that. Can lead to all sorts of probs."

"Oh you mean devil, Shee! Leave 'em alone."

"Long before your time, so I hear tell, when buses had things called conductors, a husband and wife were working on the same bus, he as the driver, she as the conductress. They'd had a row at home and it simmered on at work until a real bust up came. Whereupon he walked off leaving the bus, his wife and all the passengers stranded!"

"Shee, you're making it up. You pain you!" And they fell about laughing. "Anyway, when you's gonna invite Willie home so I can meet him. You know I want to. I'll do us all a great meal."

"Too difficult, Kats. That's what I mean, mixing business and pleasure."

"Aw Shee, come on. You know I'm dying to see your Willie …."

"Perhaps, on reflection, you could re-phrase that, Kats."

"Re-phrase …. what … oh, oh …. yes … I see," and once again laughter engulfed them until they were overcome with pleasure and melted into each other's arms and that most delightful of occupations for lovers, a passionate kiss.

Sheelagh rarely mentioned any cases in detail. It wasn't the done thing, but Katie wished she could share her problems more openly as she longed to comfort in times of stress, of which there were plenty for a police officer.

And the DCI was going to be facing stress in the form of 'amateur' interference any time soon. Dealing with the murder of Gareth Modlum she'd come up against Ernest Pawden, a fan of crime novels, who'd organised his neighbours into a kind of posse to try and find out where a suspect lived. And succeeded. Now, as yet unbeknown to both women, the DCI was going to come up against Edith Footlong who was on the verge of launching her own investigation. And that was without any input from crafty Sally Cainton who was also set to become a thorn in Sheelagh's side.

***

47

Edith Footlong had no interest in crime novels or TV crime for that matter and would've been horrified to discover that her interest in the murder of Alana Merde was about to escalate into something more detailed. But that was what fate had in store for her, and in this Grace Cathcart was to be a driving force.

For now the two ladies were revelling in the pleasure their afternoon tea the previous day had bought them. What wonderful memories!

Someone else delving into memories was Ken Waghorn, but his recollections gave him no pleasure whatsoever. His dear wife was long gone, taken by cancer which thrust its way into their lives without notice and tore them to pieces as it did for many people. He'd been at her bedside in the hospice when she passed away, all the pain and agony gone in one dreadful moment. He had prayed to a God he didn't believe in for her release, was happy when that release came, but was utterly devastated by his loss.

She was so young, really. Too young, surely? Fifty-eight, no age at all. Today he was simply a lonely old man, and that loneliness had led to stupidity unbecoming a gentleman. In a small village gossip spread like wildfire and people were talking too freely about his assignations with Alana, talk that was bound to reach her husband's ears. And then what? Well, he only had himself to blame. He found himself hoping that he hadn't been indirectly responsible for her demise, that Carl hadn't learned of her indiscretions and taken revenge.

Secretly he hoped Carl would soon be locked up so that he might be safe, but he also knew he hoped the man was not guilty and that the police would find the real perpetrator. Confusing thoughts indeed.

Carl Merde was not a man without emotions, far from it, but he had been taught from a young age that men don't cry. His father had once beaten him after warning that if he made any noise or cried he would be beaten again. He made no sound, no tears fell. And so he entered adult life knowing his must never make any fuss, show his true feelings, get emotional, or give in to pain which must be ignored.

Alana was his one and only. He'd not been able to form any lasting attachments thanks to his upbringing but Alana had been so kind and understanding, and he'd worshipped her without realising she was counting her blessings in a different way. Here was man she could effectively enslave, who would do her every bidding, for here was a man with no other chance of a wife who would not want to lose this once-in-lifetime opportunity.

And so it proved to be.

***

Meantime a kind of nemesis was homing in on Ken Waghorn. Even now Sally Cainton was nearing his doorstep and in first-degree readiness for her act. This had to be an Oscar winning performance! As he opened the door her sad, doleful eyes looked up at him pleadingly. She had taken care to position herself down a couple of steps so that he wouldn't feel threatened.

"Hello Mr Waghorn," she said in her best little-girl-lost voice, "it's alright, I'll be away, just wanted to say sorry for any distress I've caused you. I am truly sorry, thought I was simply doing my job, but it's gone wrong I know, and I'm very sorry.... " and a little tear slipped out of one eye and rolled down her cheek. "I'll be away now, won't trouble you again...." and she paused hopefully, and was rewarded.

"Look Miss Cainton ...."

"It's Sally, Mr Waghorn."

"Well Sally, I realise you were just doing your job, and I'm Ken by the way, but let's at least part as friends. We can't talk out here, please come in if you have a few moments to spare."

Bingo!

The spider had spun her web and the fly was caught in it.

Chapter Ten

It was time to hypothesise, and DS Lucy Panshaw was in the proverbial chair accompanied by DC Hassana Achebe and DC Sian Stramer. Lucy spoke first.

"Right, if it wasn't Carl then it had to be an intruder. The side gate would appear to be the obvious point of entry especially as it wasn't bolted. According to Carl he brought the wheelie-bin in and must've forgotten to bolt the gate. Now I don't like that. If I'd brought a bin in and stopped to close the gate I'm sure I'd have secured the bolts at the same time.

"Bolts top and bottom. The only other way an intruder could be there would be by climbing the fences, either at the foot of the garden or from the neighbours' gardens. Both neighbours have security lights that, when activated, set off the CCTV cameras and we've checked, neither was called upon. The Merdes had no security lights, let alone CCTV.

"The problem with the side gate theory is that the intruder would not have expected the gate to be unbolted. Yes, you could climb up and reach over and undo the top one, we checked, but there's no access to the bottom one, there being less than two centimetres under the gate. So it seems to me that the back fence is the most likely. Any thoughts guys?" Hassana was ready with her own theory and enthusiastically waiting her chance to speak.

"Here's a thought. Suppose, just suppose, this was an arranged meeting, not that Alana expected to be killed, of course. She agreed to meet someone on the patio around a certain time and had told them the side gate would be unbolted. We gather Alana crept out of bed, down the stairs and out onto the patio via the lounge. Now, if you wondered if you'd got an intruder wouldn't you wake your husband? Would you go out alone in the dark all by yourself? Yes, I know these are enlightened times for us girls, but even so, especially a woman of Alana's age, no I don't buy it. Also, wouldn't you put a dressing gown or similar on, not just slip out the back in next to nothing?

"So what was the meeting about? Handing something over, perhaps? Maybe Alana didn't have what the caller wanted and was stabbed as a consequence. Possibly she was going to die anyway."

"Blimey Hassana, you make it sound like a gangland killing," exclaimed Lucy.

"Want to know my theory?" chirruped Sian, determined not to be left out. "We've been puzzled by the position the body was left in. If Hassana is right then it could be taken as a sign that she'd double-crossed someone. You know, arms out wide, one cross, legs wide apart, second cross. A double-crossing if you follow me." Lucy and Hassana did but the DS didn't take to it.

"Well, you two are making a drama out of this! But I'm pleased you're thinking outside the box. Anything else? Sian didn't hesitate.

"Carl. Did he perhaps witness the killing? If our theory's anything like correct was he there? Were they both into something illegal? Did they ignore the killer's warnings and Alana paid the price?"

"Hold on, hold on," Lucy interrupted, "if both of them were involved why meet the other person round the back? Why not invite your caller through the front door?"

"Too much chance of being seen," Hassana intervened. Lucy nodded, wondering why she hadn't thought of that. Hassana continued: "Besides whizzing through the side gate and walking round the back, just as easy." Lucy nodded again and Sian did too.

"Okay, guys, now I've got to go and put this to our beloved leader and try and avoid a nuclear fallout if she thinks it's as daft as it sounds. Jeez. Don't' fancy my chances….. "

*****

Elsewhere a very nervous, extremely red-faced young man, was desperately and painfully trying to explain himself. And failing. PC Thomas Bowlman was standing in front of Willie Broughton who was, quite frankly, enjoying himself toying with the rookie's embarrassment.

"Thought you ought to know sir. Chanced upon it, like. Wasn't really looking …. well, not looking for that sort of thing … you know …. I'm not interested in … ummm ….well, I wouldn't ... even if I could afford it and I ... er .... can't. Doesn't appeal to me, that sort of thing, and I shouldn't have been looking ... but .... but there it was ..... I mean, there she was. Sir."

"Who?"

"From the village, sir. Francesca Towford, sir."

"And what exactly was Francesca Towford doing on this website you inadvertently stumbled upon?"

"Er .... advertising, sir."

"Advertising what, Constable?"

"Ummm .... herself, sir, if you follow me, sir."

"Herself? What was she selling? Is she a cleaner, a carer, what precisely?"

"She's a high class .... high class ....high class ...."

"If it helps, Thomas, the old-fashioned word is courtesan." Thomas sighed with relief, and, unable to contain himself any longer, Willie burst into laughter while the Constable went beetroot red. "Sorry mate, been playing you along. Loosen up and smile. Don't worry, your secret's safe with me!"

"Oh ... right ....oh," and his face was lowered into his chest which made Willie laugh all the more.

"Look Thomas, I'm really sorry. I have done the dirty on you and I'm sorry. Not the behaviour of a senior officer and I'm ashamed. Please forgive." Willie was considering that if Thomas made a complaint he could be for the high jump. "Do you think this intelligence you've come by makes Francesca a murderer?" Thomas looked up again, his visage returning to its normal colour.

"Might do, sir. If it's not Carl it's somebody else, and it seems Francesca has a dark side."

"Very true, very true. Thanks for the info. I know telling me hasn't been easy, especially with my thoughtlessness," Willie still being conscious of the fact he hadn't treated Thomas well, "but tell me, does she have a trade-name, a nom-de-bed?" At last Thomas smiled.

"Yes sir. Fanny McAdams."

***

Sally Cainton left Ken Waghorn's house is possession of three items of interest to her. Yes, he'd been turned on by Sally's appearance; no, he hadn't tried his luck with any other ladies, and, in order to deflect attention from himself, he had sunk Nancy Harmand in it.

He was confident Nancy had, at various times, been Peter Pilchard's bit-on-the-side, as he termed it, and that Peter, like himself, had visited Alana Merde when Carl Merde wasn't at home. Given her skill with reading body language, facial expressions, voice patterns and so on, she'd deduced the Peter/Nancy story was probably true, but the Peter/Alana tale was nonsense. She believed him that he himself hadn't seen any other women, and could tell that her 'super-feminine' approach had won him over, to the point where she might be welcomed again in the future.

They parted good friends, Ken unaware he had nurtured a viper to his bosom.

***

Edith Footlong was engrossed in her map of the village and all the notes she'd appended to it, as well as all the detail in her notebook. She decided she fancied a walk despite the heat of the day. Her intention was to arrive at an accurate visual picture to go with the map, so her notebook went with her, although she knew she would have to be surreptitious about writing anything while out. A chance meeting was to change the whole purpose of the excursion.

She just happened to be strolling past the Merdes house when Carl appeared in the front garden. For a second they both stopped still and stared at each other. Edith had to think quickly.

"Hello Mr Merde. I'm Mrs Footling, Edith Footlong. We don't know each other than as fellow villagers but I'd like to say how sorry I was to hear of your sad loss ...."

"Yeah, and you reckon I did it, don't you, just like the rest of them."

"No I don't, that is, you haven't been charged, have you, and I accept that the police must be looking for someone else. I haven't condemned you. It must've been a terrible shock and I really am sorry, believe me I am." The rage etched in his face eased as he tried to weigh up the situation in front of him. Could she be genuine?

"She was the love of my life. Yes, led me a merry dance, I'll admit that. But I loved her. I didn't kill her, not my little ….. well, not the woman I loved. There, that good enough for you?"

"I believe you Mr Merde. I lost my husband a few short years ago, just as we should've been setting about enjoying our retirement, and I miss him so, and while I didn't have to endure finding him stabbed to death his demise was as shocking and painful as your loss must've been." Carl managed to feel a little remorse for his rough words. A little remorse, but not much.

"Sorry Mrs Footlong."

"Edith."

"Thanks, and I'm Carl. Fancy a chat over a cuppa Edith. Give all these bast …. sorry, other people, something to gossip about. Bloody gossip, all they do all day. Show me you're different." Edith could hardly refuse such an eloquently put invitation, bearing in mind it had the added advantage of the opportunity to get to know the number one suspect.

"Yes, love to Carl. Thanks. And yes, I'd love to give them all a new topic of conversation for I am well-versed in the processes of village rumour and would be quite delighted to be at the centre of it for once!"

Chapter Eleven

Grace was entering into the spirit of killer hunting and looking for culpability where it might not exist, unaware her partner in sleuthing was at that very moment chatting to the number one suspect.

Mmm … she thought, I'd like to know more about Donald Parkforth and Belinda Thredsham, a couple who seemed to have it all and have ended up as if they'd suffered a huge financial loss. Fancy Edith not knowing they weren't married! Called their property Falconwood: now, there's no woodland nearby and we only occasionally glimpse a falcon, so a curious choice. Perhaps, coming from Rainham, they thought it sounded rural and maybe they are keen ornithologists, with a particular interest in birds of prey. Mmmm …

I wouldn't make a good bird lover, she mused, as I adore seeing the male sparrowhawk swoop over the fence, low down, to take its prey. Nature at work. But then I like the magpies too, amongst the most beautiful of birds, yet they are detested because they take other birds eggs. But it's just nature. After all, we eat those little lambs we see, or at least some of us do. Don't think I could ever be a vulcan or whatever the word is, like my roast beef too much!

But I digress. Now, where was I? Oh yes, then there's Miss Towford, although I expect she prefers to by termed Mzzz. Wouldn't suit me, I'm proud to me called Mrs. Anyway, I'm wandering off the beaten track again. According to Mrs Trumpling she has a mysterious side and that might well be the case, I mean, a part-time supermarket worker with a house in the country and a snazzy car? Suspicious!

Then there's Mr Digbin; never liked the man, a bit abrupt for my liking, and I'm sure he beats his wife. Should be a hanging offence in my book. Mr Merde was seen visiting her while Mr Digbin was driving his train or whatever he does with it, so is there an obscure connection there? F'rinstance, if Mr Digbin had found out his wife was seeing someone else not only might he take it out on Mrs Digbin, he might seek revenge elsewhere. I'm certain he's the sort.

Not sure about Mr Bargeman, but he's on my list because he's often away from home, and might have a dark side. Mrs B quite publicly warned villagers off using Mr Merde as a carpenter, so did Mr Merde threaten her or something, and Mr B taught him a lesson by killing his wife? No, that's far-fetched, but I suppose people have been killed for less.

It's the same with the Pilchards. Something fishy about them … oh dear … I've made a funny. Must remember to tell Edith that one. Men being men again; he gets mixed up with Mrs Harmand, naughty boy, so did he get mixed up with Mrs Merde and Mrs Pilchard killed her? But then again she'd have gone after Mrs Harmand as well, wouldn't she? My goodness me, we might have had a whole lot of murders being committed here, and none of us would be safe.

Now let me think, is there anybody else?

***

The heat was doing its best to strangle the life out of the Kent countryside, hosepipe bans were coming, and everywhere looked tired and worn out. It was hot. Heatwave territory. For some humid, sleepless nights took hold, bringing with them breathlessness that was almost stifling. But for many summer weather in the summer was there to be enjoyed and the county's roads were flooded, not with water, but with vehicles heading for the coast.

Kent enjoys a special situation being effectively surrounded on three sides by water, so the number of coastal destinations, and their variety, is substantial. Edith learned that Carl Merde had been a frequent holidaymaker in Kent right from his childhood so she was surprised he had retired to an inland village.

"Like this, Edith. You can do things to death …. oh, that was a daft thing to say, never mind. Me and Alana were always down here, on caravan and holiday parks, and it got a bit same-ish, know what I mean? Been nice to get away from it all. The family can always come and visit, you know, Albert and Stephen and their children and that. Alana loved having them down, but I was the one who had to arrange it, you know, Mr Fix-it and all that, and sometimes I had to get aggressive to make them come, give 'em a real bol …. telling off, know what I mean? If they tried to wriggle out I was the one who had to kind of persuade them, if you know what I mean."

He's a one-man conversation, Edith decided. He hasn't stopped talking. He's got the Merde Mouth, she christened it. I wonder if Alana got a word in edgeways? Probably did, if she wanted something done! Eventually, Edith took a chance.

"If you want to talk about that night, if it would help, I'd be prepared to listen. I don't suppose you've had much chance to talk about your thoughts and feelings, and I'm neutral in a way, not police, not family, and I'm not hostile!" He smiled, considered his position, concluded he'd got nothing to lose, and started telling his story.

"Well, you know what it's like being an oldie. Oh, sorry, didn't mean that personally. You know, nights are difficult sometimes, in and out of bed for a sl ….. for the toilet. Well, I was dog-tired and I fell asleep after one of these visits and I swear I didn't know Alana got out of the bed. When I woke and she wasn't there, well, after a while I called out. No reply. Called again. No reply. So I got up, put my dressing gown on and went to the bathroom. No sign.

"So I went downstairs calling out to her. No reply, so by now I was well worried I can tell you. And when I went in the lounge I saw the open patio door and her lying on the deck. I thought she'd had a heart attack or something and rushed over. Then I stopped dead. Oh blimey, me and my words! Stopped in my tracks. I'll never forget that moment Edith, know what I mean? I saw the knife even though it was dark and everything else ceased to mean anything. There was my wife, stabbed and I didn't know what to do. I almost rushed over but I don't know anything about feeling for a pulse. I don't know why, I couldn't go out there, I stumbled around and put a light on in the lounge, and left her there in the dark.

"But the worst of it was, and I can't live with myself over this, I couldn't touch her. It was like she was an alien being. So I dashed to the 'phone and dialled 999, asked for police and ambulance. They told me to look for signs of breathing. I went back to her and I still couldn't get near, and then I broke down completely. But I knew she was dead. Her chest wasn't going up and down for one thing.

"When they all turned up they was kind at first but then the police got the idea I must've done it. I mean, stab my beautiful baby? No way. But it's been a nightmare since." At this point the Merde-Mouth came to a halt and Carl looked down at the floor. Edith was perceptive enough to realise he wanted to cry heartily and that something was preventing him. Did he belong to the school of thought that said grown men don't cry? She went quietly and sat next to him and whispered.

"It's alright Carl. Just the two of us and I won't talk. I know you didn't do it. You'll feel so much better if you let those tears fall. It will help you, it will."

After a couple of minutes of silence he suddenly burst into tears, a fearsome torrent, heaving shoulders, pathetic cries of pain, agony personified. God, thought Edith, he's wanted to do this and something's stopped him. It's crazy. It helps to show your true feelings, and maybe he hasn't shown this side of him to the police. It would be easy to imagine that he had no love for Alana and wasn't missing her. But he was, and Edith knew it. All this time and he'd just wanted someone to talk to, just wanted to be able to show those feelings, and had kept them all sealed up inside him. Small wonder he thought everyone was against him and viewed him as guilty.

But at the same time she knew, really *knew* he wasn't the killer. And she felt renewed enthusiasm for delving into Little Scampering's occupants, and who knew? She might uncover the murderer. Perhaps now she owed it to Carl and to Alana's memory.

***

Harry and Lizzie Thrack had decided they'd debated the issue far too much and now rarely spoke of the matter, much to the relief of their offspring.

"Aw, leave it out, the pair of you," the youngest had cried, fed up with murder, murder, murder and not much else, "let's talk about something interesting like music and gaming." And so on.

After tea the Thrack's spoke about how Kent had changed, about the weather and about how things used to be in the good-old-days. Their teenage children were unimpressed and drifted off to find other pleasurable pursuits befitting their own interests. Mum and dad didn't believe in climate change and how humans had damaged the planet, and they disagreed with the idea of making cannabis legal. They didn't like the music of Adele, didn't understand, or want to understand the benefits of true socialism, and thought their children too young to be able to make big decisions in their lives. Parents! Who'd have 'em!

The Thracks were not the only ones calling time on Alana Merde's demise. Fewer people were gossiping about it and other topics of conversation were arising. In this, however, the scope had been initially provided by the murder, and fuelled by gossip and the efforts of the reporter, Sally Cainton. She was currently heading in the direction of Nancy Harmand with every intention of stirring up trouble in the hope of landing a worthwhile story, even if it had nothing or very little to do with the death.

Sally, with the agreement of her editor, had moved her own goalposts. The feature she saw unfolding before her was an expose of life in a sleepy little village, with all the undercurrents of sleaze, spite, envy, jealousy, enduring friendship and love and lust brought to the surface, none of this normally visible to the naked eye. What a story! Village life in the raw. She saw Little Scampering as a hotbed of hidden tales just waiting to be thrust into the limelight.

Nobody would ever look upon our beautiful idyllic villages in the same way again!

Unfortunately, this new angle of attack was to have a downside, and a potentially lethal one too. For by digging in this direction Sally was going to put her life in danger.

***

"What?" The one-word question was softly spoken. The second one was almost shrieked.

"*What?*" cried the DCI. Lucy Panshaw was used to these reactions and had been persuaded they were a professional way of trying to make 'underlings' as the DCI always termed them

59

feel insignificant. And wrong. Lucy, since her promotion to Detective Sergeant, had determined that she would stand her ground in such exchanges and, to a degree, trust that being a woman would save her from the worst of the storm, a pleasure routinely denied Willie Broughton for obvious reasons.

"Okay, okay, I'll buy the idea it might have been a pre-arranged meeting," Sheelagh was calming and relaxing and thinking, "as that might explain the unbolted gate. But the rest of it, Lucy? I would suggest to you that arms out wide and legs akimbo would constitute one cross only." Both women dissolved into chuckles. "But no, we've got to explore all avenues, despite my money being on Carl. Go grill him, Lucy, and watch his reaction carefully. Oh, I don't need to tell you all this. Put your theories to him, frighten him some. Take Hassana or Sian. Keep him worried."

Chapter Twelve

Edith's back garden was north-facing so that her patio was mainly in shade as the day wore on. It was the ideal spot to entertain Grace for some tea and she'd made some salmon and cucumber sandwiches for the purpose. Mid-July had barely passed and the predicted heatwave was approaching together with all the attendant Met Office warnings. Neither lady was looking forward to it, not one jot. This was hot enough today without temperatures reaching 40 Celsius or more.

However, there was much to talk about and it helped take their minds off their discomfort. Grace checked her own notes which she'd brought with her and put her concerns to Edith.

"I don't know why, but I'm bothered about Donald Parkforth and his partner, Belinda. Such a strange thing, Edith, but why I should worry about the name they gave the property, I don't know. Falconwood sounds rural enough, especially if you've lived in town."

"Wait a minute, Grace, Falconwood, that rings a bell. If my geography's correct there's a Falconwood in south-east London, and not far from Eltham, where the Merdes came from. Do we know for sure Donald Parkforth came from Rainham?"

"No, good point, we don't. It's just what he told people. But that might be genuine if they moved there from Falconwood in the first place. Are you suggesting, Edith, there might be a connection between them and the Merdes? And that something might have happened between them?"

"You're very perceptive, Grace," and both ladies smiled, Grace because she appreciated the light sarcasm and accepted it as harmless humour, and Edith because no offence had been intended, a remark made purely in jest. "But we mustn't read too much into it and get carried away."

"No, you're quite right. Spoilsport." This time they giggled then paused for more sandwiches and for some of Edith's excellent chilled fresh fruit juice. "Now, let's turn to Miss Towford …."

"I think we can dismiss her, Grace. We'd all like to know where the money's come from and what she's up to …."

"Yes, but Edith, suppose Alana found out and threatened to tell everyone and … and … and tried to blackmail her." Grace was becoming breathless with excitement.

"If all she does is keep herself to herself, and doesn't want to explain her finances, we shouldn't assume there's anything bad or illegal about them."

"Are you going to pooh-pooh all my ideas, Edith?"

"Good heavens no. Now, let's discuss the Digbins and the Pilchards, come on." Edith was anxious to divert her friend from despondency, but realised Grace was now seeing potential evil everywhere, confirmation coming when Mrs Cathcart started expounding her views on the other two couples and doing so with increased fervour.

***

There had been a police presence in the village right from the start, but now this was confined to one or two uniformed officers primarily to keep a close eye on Mr Merde, but also to engage with villagers where this might be beneficial.

The diminutive figure of PC Thomas Bowlman was a frequent sight along the lane where he often stopped for a chat with anyone who might be abroad or out in their front garden. With the excessive heat most felt sorry for him but a caring few would offer a cold drink, Poojah Nagarka among them. She was happy to natter to him, learned a great deal about him and, in his turn, he discovered much about her part of India and her career as a nurse. He'd asked her about her ambitions when she was young and found she had a simple philosophy.

"Well, Thomas, I knew from a young age who I would be married to and I accepted that as it was our way of life. Deepak lived in the next village so I knew him from childhood and liked him. I wanted to help people and had the remarkable opportunity to come to England to train in the medical profession, as Deepak did, although we came at separate times.

"We view life in a comparatively simple way. Our calling was to help people by using medicine and I decided I wanted to be a nurse so that I was always in contact with the people who needed help. And that is how, eventually, I ended up in a nursing home. I had no ambitions to become a senior nurse or to develop a career because I was answering my calling and I was dedicated to it. I have happiness and contentment, Thomas, as has Deepak. There has no been pressure beyond doing what we wanted to do, that is, help people, make sick people better. But I suspect you are a man of ambition, Thomas, are you not?" The young officer now felt embarrassed.

"Mmm, well, Mrs Nagarka," he spoke to her formally as he believed that was right and proper, as his dad would've said, and he had politely declined her invitation to use her forename, "the fact is, yes, I'd like to be a detective and I'd like to get on, get promoted. Not quite your philosophy is it, Mrs Nagarka?"

"No, but in a way it is a parallel. You want to catch criminals, protect the public, it is your own calling, and I admire you, and like many young people you want to get on in life. I do not say you are wrong. I view life differently but respect those who view it in other ways. I respect everyone's right to an opinion." Thomas could've talked all day to this woman with a refreshing attitude but it was time to move on, so he thanked her for the drink, said farewell and set off with much to think about.

One thing for sure, it was inconceivable that either Mr or Mrs Nagarka could've murdered anyone! Then the policeman in him caught up. You can't discount anyone; to do so might be to overlook the truth. And he found the conflict of thoughts was hurting him. Nobody dedicated to curing the sick could take life so violently, surely?

***

A man with a rather dissimilar approach to life was Peter Digbin. He fully supported strike action in pursuit of a better wage settlement and had wangled a local job on strike days, cash-in-hand. As a lad he'd always wanted to be a train driver despite the fact his parents had done their level best to dissuade him from such a venture, and had thoroughly enjoyed his employment once he'd qualified. Based at Gillingham he mainly drove the commuter routes between there and London.

He hadn't been able to confirm the rumours about his wife seeing Carl Merde. She'd utterly denied it even when he'd been punching her to the ground. As a bully he felt that as she'd withstood such treatment she must be telling the truth, whereas she was hiding a guilty secret and was prepared to be thrashed in this abominable manner, knowing Peter would stop when he thought he'd won.

Carl wasn't attractive in any way, shape or form, but he'd shown a degree of kindness that was missing in her miserable life, and it was only friendship. His rare visits had been seen, someone had spilled the beans to that reporter, and Peter had exploded as he usually did. Was every marriage like this, she wondered?

She'd met Carl when he was walking past and she was tending a plant in the front garden. His cheery 'hello' was too much on that particular day and she'd burst into tears. From such small beginnings was much comfort forthcoming. Carl had told her his wife was a basket, his term, a pampered pooch, who didn't have a kind bone in her body. For her part Alison told him about the beatings.

"You don't have to put up with that, love. Right out of order. Not right, it ain't. I'll come and sort him if you like….."

"No, no, no," she'd whimpered, "it'll only make it worse."

And so these two sad people found something precious with each other, something that was missing from their sorrowful lives. Alison came to long for these occasional meetings, and Carl knew he had at last found someone who treasured him for himself, and both were suffering the anguish of knowing they could never get closer, and the pain of knowing their relationship, of necessity, was doomed. Two wounded souls destined for a horrible nothingness.

***

Sally Cainton had not been surprised by her reception at Nancy Harmand's. She was instructed, most impolitely, where she should go and, perhaps impertinently, what she should do when she got there. Sally had heard it all before so was completely unfazed. But from a supposedly genteel retired lady?

64

And they said Carl Merde could be obnoxious in his choice of language!

Nancy was seething. She'd enjoyed her dalliance with Kevin Pilchard, exciting him in ways his wife clearly could not manage, but it had ended when he confessed to Kathy because he valued his marriage too much. Nancy had always accepted the affair was going nowhere and would cease abruptly, but had assumed that it was not gossip-worthy even in a small village, and would vanish into the ether somewhere to be forgotten.

Careful though they had been, their meetings, which might have been quite innocent but weren't, had been observed and now a nasty person had sunk them in it, making the business effectively public. Who could it be?

The Pilchards were next on Sally's list.

"Hello, Mrs Pilchard? Sally Cainton …." and that was as far as she got, the door slammed in her face. "Well thank you. Let me tell you," she explained to the front door, "that this is one big shark after you, Mrs Pilchard, and I have my teeth into you and your husband and I'm not letting go." Kathy Pilchard was already 'phoning the police on the number they'd all been given and was eventually put through to Willie in the Incident Room. Eventually, because it was quite a wait and no, she didn't want to leave a message. "God," she exclaimed, "even the police are at it. My call is important to them, of course it bloody isn't or you'd answer it," she yelled while Kevin diplomatically kept out of the way.

Willie listened patiently then asked the inevitable question and in doing so lit the blue touch paper.

"Mrs Pilchard, why does Sally Cainton want to speak to you. What interests her?" Kathy blustered and stuttered as she tried to think quickly.

"Oh, I expect she's heard some rumour about us. There's so much gossip here and we've got neighbours shopping neighbours as I expect you're only too aware."

"No, we're not, Mrs Pilchard. Nobody's been shopped to us. Are people spreading malicious stories about fellow villagers, or are folks afraid of hidden truths, do you think? Did you give Sally a chance to say what she wanted?"

"Not so likely, Sergeant. She's only the press and we've all had enough of them. Can't you keep them away from us?"

"If you have nothing hide, Mrs Pilchard, why not at least hear what she had to say? It might have been innocent. By the way, do you know of any tales circulating about you that put you on your guard?"

"Officer, I do not like the way you're talking to me. I'm a taxpayer and I expect a bit of respect, you know. Your attitude is bordering on the insolent and I'll be calling my local councillor next, believe me. I've rung you with a legitimate complaint about press harassment and you seem determined to have a go at me."

By now Willie had decided that, yes indeed, Mrs P had something to hide and was the subject of village gossip. Have to look into that, he thought, and no, you won't slam the door in a police officer's face.

"Mrs Pilchard, my apologies if I've offended, it was not intentional," he lied. "May I send a colleague to speak to you personally? We are taking you seriously, we truly are, and I think face-to-face is the best medium, don't you? DC Sian Stramer is in your area and she can call in if that's convenient?" Kathy calmed and replied that yes, that was a good idea, and yes, it was convenient.

Good, thought Willie. Two birds with one stone. And with a female officer who can get blood out of that stone. Me in the clear and we get to hear about another fascinating story from Little Scampering. Wonder if Carl's involved in this? And may God save us from taxpayers!

Chapter Thirteen

Lucy and Hassana were grilling Carl or, more to the point, roasting him over an open spit.

"I didn't kill my wife. Why do you keep attacking me? For God's sake. Alright, alright, so I saw Alison Digbin, so I got cosy with her. It happens, it's called life. Perhaps you don't get to see the real world, see life like it is. So yes, I spent some time with Alison. Her husband beats her, did you know that? Do you do people like that for assault, cos you ought to. Terrible, dreadful. You should've seen what he's done to her. Vicious. I'd have given him a thumping if she'd let me.

"Just for the record, and to give you something else to get after, Alana confronted that Francesca Towford woman, cos she kept running me down to everyone. I did a bit of carpentry, know what I mean, and she thought it was rubbish. Then Alana discovered she had a job on the side, never knew what, she didn't tell me. Anyway, she weren't paying tax on it. Not a crime, though I bet your lot think it is. That's where she gets all her money from. So Alana warns her. Stop running my husband down or I'll tell what I know. Have a chat with her. Perhaps she had a motive, cos I didn't. I tell you, I never killed my wife."

***

Edith was sweltering in the front garden, dead-heading the roses when PC Thomas Bowlman wandered by, in shirt sleeves but still looking over-dressed for the heat.

"Oh officer, you look so hot. Would you like a glass of ice-cold water or ice-cold apple juice?"

"Mrs Footlong, thank you, and I'd love a glass of water."

"You remembered my name then?"

"Yes, I'm good with names and faces. Handy being in the police. And I'm Thomas, everyone calls me Thomas, please do the same."

"And you are welcome to call me Edith."

"That's kind, but I won't do if it's all the same to you, Mrs Footlong. It's right and proper, me being a policeman, you being one of the people we're here to serve." What a refreshing attitude, she thought, and what a lovely gentleman.

He accepted her offer to sit in the cool indoors while he took his drink, and she decided she'd take a chance.

"Thomas, I am certain you and your colleagues are doing all they can to catch the perpetrator of this shocking crime, and I wouldn't want you to think me an interfering busy-body, but would you mind if I mentioned one thing to you? You may already be looking into this."

"I am sure I would not think ill of you in any way, Mrs Footlong, and we do rely on help from the public, so please speak." She told him succinctly about Donald Parkforth and his partner, and how they named their cottage Falconwood, and that Falconwood is not far from Eltham where the Merdes came from. Did they actually know each other and had there been a problem between them in days gone by? And might that problem have been enough to kill?"

Thomas was now almost opened mouthed, but he pulled himself together, took out his notebook and wrote down what he'd been told, promising Edith he'd tell the team as soon as he could. Somehow Edith sensed he hadn't taken her seriously, but hoped he might pursue the intelligence.

"Well, thank you Mrs Footlong. That was very kind, and thank you for your information. I'll relay that to base as soon as I'm able, but you do realise we can't discuss the outcome with you?"

Edith said that she did, and he departed to continue his patrol through the village. She observed him speaking into his radio and trusted he was contacting the team, as he called them. It was indeed exactly what he was doing.

***

DC Stramer had arrived at Nancy Harmand's, and in another matter DS Willie Broughton was trying not to laugh. Sian introduced herself but was not immediately admitted until she pointed out that conducting an interview on the doorstep might arouse further rumour in a community awash with gossip. Willie was in the Incident Room reading the information supplied by PC Bowlman, and it was even funnier the second time round. But his policeman's brain came to the rescue and he took a deep breath and decided to initiate enquiries, leaving the humour locked away where it should've been from the outset. This was, after all, a murder investigation.

First of all he radioed Hassana who had been sitting quietly, the agreed procedure, while Lucy had tackled Carl. She excused herself, went to the kitchen and received the message, returned to the lounge and signalled to Lucy she wanted to speak to Carl.

Nancy Harmand, meanwhile, with her back up at the intrusion, was using attack as the best form of defence, and explaining in unnecessary detail the affair she'd had with Kevin Pilchard. Sian would rather have been spared the intimate descriptions, especially as she found it all rather boring, and decided to interrupt her host while she was in full flow.

"Thank you, Mrs Harmand. Tell me, have you had affairs with any other villagers. Carl Merde for example." Nancy looked shocked.

"None of your business. You've asked me about Kevin….."

"It is our business. We looking into a cruel murder. We'll ask any questions we like."

"Well, really!"

"And the answer is ….?"

"No, officer. Nobody else. My husband died at the age of fifty-five. I've managed quite well without anyone else. He was my one true love. Kevin happened out of the blue and I thoroughly enjoyed it because I knew nothing would come of it, he being married, and now it's over, and I don't need to dabble again. Is there anything else you'd like to know about my private life, as if not I'm busy and I'd like you to leave."

"Thank you, Mrs Harmand, You've been most helpful. I'll show myself out. Goodbye."

***

"No, not known them before. I did a bit of work up there, before my name was blackened, but that was the first time I'd met them. Thought they came from Rainham, least that's what they told me." Carl was answering Hassana's questions about Donald Parkforth, and his attitude suggested his replies were genuine.

"We wondered if they in fact came from Falconwood, even if they moved to Rainham first." He didn't bat the proverbial eyelid, but did shrug his shoulders.

"No idea, love. They weren't very talkative, I had to do all the talking." Yes, thought Lucy, I expect you did!

Just along the lane Sian had arrived at the Pilchards' and been hurriedly escorted to the lounge with the front door shut briskly behind her, a complete contrast to her welcome at Nancy Harmands.

Kevin was sitting in an armchair and was pleased and relieved when asked to go and rustle up some cold drinks, an exercise he took his time with. Kathy hastily explained what she described as the 'gory details' of her husband's affair, although there was nothing gory to be related, and went on to plead for protection from the media who wanted to hound her over a rumour. Hardly a rumour, Sian thought.

"We'll talk to the editor, Mrs Pilchard, and it does worry me that this reporter's enquiries have little to do with the murder of Mrs Merde. I should say she's chasing stories around the village, not trying to find a killer, like, but we'll find out, rest assured. If she troubles you again give me a call, and please leave a message, like, if you can't get through to me. I'll get it as soon as I can, believe me." Kevin appeared with a tray of glasses, a jug of squash with the obligatory ice-cubes, and the three of them sat back to enjoy their refreshments, Kathy having calmed considerably.

"Sorry to have to ask this, but this *is* related to the murder," Sian began, "and I need to know if you had any sort of relationship with the dead woman. Sorry, but I have to ask."

Kathy spluttered into her drink, Kevin reddened and then spoke, almost in a whisper.

"No, there's been nobody else. I've been a stupid man, regret what I did, and I have to live knowing I betrayed Kathy." Sian was watching him and felt he was telling the truth.

"I've seen her online photos Willie, and no, I am not sending you to interview Fanny McAdams as not only will you return in about three days time, you'll be half the man you are and that isn't saying much, plus you will be broke, and not only financially!"

"Aw ma'am, thought I'd be ideal …."

"Why do men think they are the answer to every woman's prayers? You'd certainly be the answer to her flagging bank balance, I'll grant you that. Not that she's likely to be in overdraft. No, I'll get Lucy to call. Now go and have a cold shower then we'll talk about the case."

Chapter Fourteen

Little Scampering had become something of a macabre tourist attraction since the murder and business at the *Downsman* was booming, much to the delight of the landlords, Eric and Felicity Trumpling. Of course, this was in part down to the exceptional weather and the baking conditions frazzling humans and the countryside alike, and many humans were heading for watering holes like the village pub during this traditional holiday season.

Felicity rather regretted not realising her dream to provide accommodation but that had been shattered by the pandemic, and its restoration was an improbability given the general financial situation all round. She and one of the barmaids, Abigail Laindon, had become adept at creating and helping to spread rumours relating to life in the village in general and the murder in particular, and it was all lapped up by visitors.

Using her well-honed skills Felicity could start a brief story, whet the listeners appetite, and then pause until they'd finished their drink and bought another one, before resuming the fascinating tale. She and Abigail bounced off each other with aplomb and made the gossip even more exciting and intriguing. And thirsty work for drinkers, they made sure of that!

Unfortunately, they were given to getting carried away, and often maligned locals in a manner that could be termed slanderous, and therefore potentially actionable had their victims wished to pursue redress.

Once upon a time Sally Cainton frequented the pub but had come to the conclusion there was nothing to be gained these days, and was aware Felicity and Abigail were manufacturing nonsense which might easily waste her time. Best to go it alone. She tried a couple of houses nearby without any success and then came upon Falconwood. Belinda opened the door.

"Hello, sorry to trouble you, I'm Sally Cainton from …."

"Yes, I know. You called before. I've nothing to add. Sorry, but I'm busy."

"I'm truly sorry to have disturbed you. Thanks anyway. Just out of interest I see your home is called Falconwood, any connection with the place in London?"

"Had the name when we came. Decided to keep it. Where's this Falconwood anyway?"

"South-east London."

"Wouldn't know. We moved here from Rainham. Before that, Lancashire. Thought the accent might've been a give-away. Right, no need for you to call again. Cheerio." And the door was slammed shut. Mmm … Sally mused, if I keep going at this rate most of the front doors in Little Scampering will be hanging off their hinges!

"Hello, you're from the paper, aren't you?" Sally was just through the front gate and was taken by surprise, spinning round in the direction of the voice. She had to shield her eyes from the sunlight and regretted leaving her sunglasses in the car, but recognised the lady before her.

"Oh hello, you're Mrs Cathcart, aren't you?"

"That's me. What a good memory you have."

"Need it in my profession."

"Oh yes, I expect so. Were you interviewing Mr Parkforth just now? I must say it's all getting very intriguing, isn't it?"

"No, a lady, presumably Mrs Parkforth. She couldn't wait to be rid of me."

"Oh, that's actually Miss Thredsham, Mr Parkforth's partner, and it might be Mrs Thredsham for all I know. They've not been here long."

"That's right, I remember now, you've lived here all your life." Grace nodded as they strolled into some shade on the opposite side of the road. "I was just asking Miss Thredsham about the name of the property. Falconwood. Just wondered if it had any connection with the Falconwood in London, but apparently it was the name the place had when they came here."

"No, no, that's not right. It was the village stores. It didn't have a name till they named it. But funny you should mention it because we, that is, me and Mrs Footlong, had pondered if there was a connection, what with the Merdes coming from Eltham." Sally's ears pricked up. She'd forgotten that. A new lead at last.

73

And Miss Thredsham had lied about the name of their home. What else might she have lied about? Time to investigate.

"We did tell the police but we haven't heard anything. Don't suppose it was very important."

"Well, Mrs Cathcart, I'll tell you what. I'll make some enquiries and I *will* let you know how I get on, and that's a promise!" They smiled at each other, Grace supplied her address and telephone number, and then they parted company. Must tell Edith, she thought to herself as she quickened her step in Edith's direction.

***

Rather than a cold shower Willie Broughton settled for cold water to drink and brought his boss one back from the machine.

"Apple for teacher, eh?" Sheelagh commented, face full of mischief. "Okay, let's go. Give me a run down."

"Run down? I'll go fetch the car..."

"Any more of that and you'll have a puncture and a bent crankshaft to contend with."

"Understood ma'am," and he bent forward in a subservient manner.

"That's more like it. Grovel. Right, down to business."

"At every turn Carl Merde looks like the killer. He was there, simples. No trace of anyone else. And let's be honest, other villagers loathed or disliked the Merdes for various reasons but surely not enough to murder." Sheelagh nodded once. "The only person we've come across that we know to be particularly violent is Peter Digbin. Yes, he might have had a reason later, if he believed the rumours about his wife, but not at the time of the murder."

"He's just a bully, Willie. I've met men like him. They love to exercise control over the only people they can master, usually the poor wife, so not likely to take on a bloke. And, let's face it, if he wanted revenge he'd have attacked Carl not Alana." Willie took his turn to nod.

"One of two minor mysteries, ma'am, such as Francesca Towford," the DCI shot him an evil glance, "and a property called Falconwood, that sort of thing. Doesn't amount to much.

Carl was the one who was detested, to various degrees, so why wasn't he the victim? I think Alana was the intended victim and if it wasn't Carl who killed her I think we're looking for an outside connection."

"Agreed, and I think we're looking beyond the realms of dislike or, indeed, hatred. So that might mean nobody in the village is involved. So it's either Carl or our other theory, that it was an arranged meeting, for whatever reason. The Merdes could've been up to their eyeballs in crime for all we know, and we need to know now Willie. How are enquiries going up Eltham way?"

"Very much in hand but nothing untoward has come to light yet."

"Okay, but give' em a gentle chase please Willie. This business is not moving at the right pace."

***

"This is disgusting. I expect you'll tell everyone what I do, now. What business is it of yours?"

"Ms Towford, I'm sorry but Carl Merde provided us with information that we need to look into. He claimed he didn't know what you were up to. Neither did we. You've just told me. He claimed his wife knew and threatened to expose you if you didn't stop denigrating his work as a carpenter. You've told us what you do, so please just answer my question. Did Alana confront you like that?"

Francesca calmed a little, just a little.

"No. I met her in the street and she asked me to stop disparaging her husband whom she clearly thought was a master carpenter. Master bodger, more like. I ignored her and walked away and that, Sergeant, is the only time we met. She never mentioned my alter ego. Does everyone have to know what I do? Will I have to move once they all know? It's disgraceful, and all because you take the word of a murderer. And that's what he is, isn't he? Pointing the finger of suspicion at me just to try and save himself."

"We have no choice when it comes to questioning you, Ms Towford, but we have no intention of publicising our results, save where a crime has been committed or someone provides vital evidence. Right now Carl Merde has not been charged which should suggest to you that we are exploring more than one avenue." Lucy made it clear the interview was over and made to leave.

"Look, Sergeant, I'm sorry. I know you're only doing your job but try and understand my position. That lying toerag has tried to implicate me because I quite correctly told people he was useless, and I'm fuming about it. Sorry. I am sorry." Lucy nodded but didn't speak. There was nothing more to say.

***

"Um … um …. do you think that was wise, Grace?"

"Why yes, Edith, she has access to more information than we could ever hope to be, and she's promised to let us know."

"But we're not investigating the crime, my dear Grace. I'm sorry to say this but think we're both getting carried away." Mrs Cathcart looked astonished at this retort.

"Edith, I'm sure neither of us is getting carried away, but you have to admit it's all become very interesting and involved and everything. Sally can look into things we can't, and I'm certain you'd like to know about Mr Parkforth and Miss Thredsham."

"I'm not convinced we should be looking into other people's lives. We wouldn't like it …."

"No, but you did tell that policeman about them, didn't you? What's the difference?"

"He's helping his colleagues unravel a major crime and he's unlikely to come and tell us the outcome of any enquiries. Sally's a reporter; they like exciting stories that sell papers. They could expose Mr Parkforth and Miss Thredsham over the slightest thing and we might've been responsible for ruining their lives."

"I hadn't thought of it like that. The police have their job to do, but a reporter can be guilty of invading someone's privacy, and no, I wouldn't like that. Alright Edith, you win. I was wrong. Now tell you what, I'll put the kettle on, we'll have a nice cuppa and we can talk about the other suspects….. "

***

If the heat was rising in the investigation it was certainly rising across Kent, with parched brown lawns decorating gardens, hosepipe bans for some, and a general feeling it was just too hot be alive. Others lapped it up, of course, and basked in the sun during this holiday season, while those going to work often struggled in the conditions.

And in the coming days DCI Sheelagh Mehedren was to be in for a surprise, and Edith and Grace were in for a shock, as things got hotter still.

Chapter Fifteen

"Sit down Willie, and don't speak," commanded she who must be obeyed, "and listen very carefully to my question. Think before you answer. Willie, answer me truthfully, the honest truth, speak freely and without fear. If you thought I was losing it, y'know, *really* losing it, would you tell me?"

"No of course I wouldn't."

"That's the right answer. You get to keep your job. Pin your ears back and hear the words of Chairman Mehedren."

"Okay, cool."

"We're just wasting time and precious resources chasing around after the villagers. They've become red herrings. In all probability Carl did it, if not it was an outside job. All these villagers who loathed the Merdes, well, they're not going to become killers overnight. I'm inclined to charge Carl because we don't have a shred of evidence anyone else was involved. Am I right?"

"Well, oh wise one, you might want to hear the news I've brought you first."

"I don't like the sound of that, mate. Okay, go ahead."

"Mmmm …. it's about villagers, ma'am. Sorry."

"Speak, my diminutive and lowly servant." Both grinned. They enjoyed a first-class working relationship built on mutual respect, admiration and high professional standards, and knew where the boundaries were and when they could cross them.

"This is where the plot *really* thickens, ma'am."

"No, this is where my patience *really* thins. Say it like it is, Willie, this isn't a television crime show, so there's no need to make a drama out of it." They were both smiling again and allowed faint chuckles to appear and to be enjoyed.

"Right. Donald Parkforth, been inside, not uno but twice. Both times fraud and serious stuff too. He comes from Bolton, by the way. Belinda Thredsham nee Reubens, also a jailbird. Two juvenile cautions for minor assaults and then a suspended sentence for a more serious attack. She's also from Lancashire, Poulton-le-Fylde, where she married local guy Rod Thredsham.

"Couple of years later they go down for drug dealing. He's out of prison just two months when he dies of a drug overdose. Must've missed it too much in prison and hit it big time on release. Anyway, the widow moves to Liverpool and meets Parkforth and disappear from view for a while, surfacing again in Wilmslow, Cheshire. They've got legit jobs but local force are watching them thinking they're up to no good, possibly drugs, possibly burglary. Then she gets caught shoplifting; suspended sentence again.

"And so they moved on. Reading, then Southend, then Aldershot and finally Rainham. Again legit jobs but not well paid ones. But they become investors in an outfit called …. wait for it …. wait for it …. Wood Falcon Developments, into all kinds of property matters. We know this because it was a scam business eventually brought down by our colleagues in Northamptonshire, where it was based. Parkforth lost a fortune, as did the other twenty or so investors who all protested their innocence and successfully so. Where he got the money, well, heaven knows. All the investors were turned over but nothing arose that could be pinned on them. Mr Wood and Mr Falcon go to prison having conned companies and people out of a hell of a lot.

"By this time Donald and Belinda had retired to Little Scampering, only to find their small fortune vanish overnight." The two detectives looked at each other in silence for several minutes.

"The other thing," Willie finally added, "about charging Carl is complete lack of forensic, ma'am. No blood on him, none on any clothing, none back in the house."

"I know, I know. Okay, get us an appointment at Falconwood, when they're *both* there, and chat to Northampton about those investors. A list of names, perhaps?"

***

Edith had met Grace around six in the morning in order to enjoy a leisurely walk along a nearby footpath before the sun became unbearable, and they were back home where Edith had prepared a delightful and tasty light breakfast of mixed fruit followed by croissants and jam washed down with coffee. Grace was looking at the previous day's paper.

"Well I never, I can't remember who is on strike at the mo. It seems to me someone is out every day. I can't keep track. I don't think the dustmen are out."

"Tut tut, Grace. You can't call them dustmen anymore. They are refuse collectors nowadays. Calling them dustmen would, I believe, be termed a hate-crime, or whatever it is, and you could be sent to prison for that." Her guest was wide-eyed with amazement.

"Good grief! You're not being serious, are you?" Her friend giggled quietly, revealing the truth. "Edith! Still, you never know these days. I wish someone would take us seriously, though. I mean, I find it offensive when people use filthy language in public, but nobody cares what offends our generation, do they Edith? We're not allowed to be offended. I cannot imagine what the world's coming to these days. So many things we can't say anymore but people can offend us and get clean away with it."

"I know. But the two of us won't change anything." They looked at each other with a simple smile of resignation and finished their coffees. "And then there's this terrible war in Ukraine and experts are saying it could go on for years. Very sad, very sad."

"I suppose, Edith, it makes this horrible business with Mrs Merde all the worse. As if there isn't enough trouble in the world without people stabbing each other, sometimes for very little reason."

"Well, let's hope the police clear it up soon, either way."

"Yes, and of course we're waiting to hear from Sally too." Grace was getting excited again and her friend sought to calm her and distract her.

"We must give her time, Grace. Now why don't you get your car out and we'll go and fetch *today's* papers?"

***

Wally and Beryl Prior were trying to ensure they kept cool all day by opening all the doors and windows to create a free flow of air, but achieved a limited result largely as there was little wind.

And it was still early.

There was a further downside to having the place so open. Carl's son Albert was staying with his father and had brought his eldest daughter with him. In the time-honoured way of the Merdes they were busy doing what comes naturally and having a blazing row which the Priors could hear quite distinctly, much to their disgust, for it was sending the filth-ometer into the red zone thanks to a stream of obscene words.

When the Merdes first moved in and subjected their neighbours to one of these heated arguments Wally later asked Carl to desist and was met with animosity liberally littered with the kind of language he had come to complain about. The relationship had started its nose-dive.

"It's too hot, Wally. The weather's getting on my nerves and I have just about had enough of them next door. You'd never believe Mrs Merde had just been brutally murdered. What a way to respect the dead."

On the other side of the Merdes at Oak View Cottage, the Sonnels could also hear the fierce altercation and were arriving at the same conclusion as the Priors. All three Merdes were at it, shouting together, not listening to each other, using foul language into the bargain.

"They've all got motor-mouths, haven't they?" Robert remarked to his wife. "Must be in the genes." Christine grinned, but it was with false humour.

"Robert, Robert, with any luck he'll move away now, especially if he goes to prison."

"Yes, but then suppose one of the sons comes to live here? I can't keep up. He seems to have so many daughters but no sign of a wife, or even a partner! Whatever are the police doing?"

***

The previous evening two of the police officers involved had been enjoying time together. Sian Stramer prepared a delicious meal for Willie Broughton. He'd loved it, but was afraid to ask what it was and show his ignorance, and endeavoured to pretend that he was fully au-fait with the dish, much to the amusement of his host who knew the difficulty he was in.

Later they relaxed in subdued lighting on a settee that all but swallowed them whole. Willie wondered how he would get up. Sian snuggled closer as they sipped at their wine, a charming Rose de Noir from Chartham Vineyard that Willie had purchased on a visit to east Kent.

"We're doing really well in Kent, y'know, with vineyards and that, eh Willie?"

"Yes, rivalling France in some cases and that's good news by me!"

"More expensive though."

"Not necessarily, not for the quality drink, like this."

"Mmmm …. and this appeals to my tastebuds just like you appeal to my lips." And they dissolved into a short but fabulous kiss as they snuggled even closer. "How many bottles of this have you, Willie?"

"Several. Who's counting? Brought two with me and this is number one."

"That's the best possible news, like, from my point of view! Sadly, I'm only a DC and I can only afford Tesco's finest!"

"What a good job you've found me, then. DS with loads of dosh, I don't think."

"Sheelagh's quite a woman. You two get on really well."

"What a team should be, and yes, she's fantastic."

"I like being on your team, Willie. Please teach me all you know." Her eyes were so full of pleading and mischief and humour that Willie was overcome, spilled his drink in the rush to get to her and reduced her to fits of the giggles, hearty giggles, soon swamped by the passion of his kisses. Sian knew, that if anything, when it came to matters of the heart, she'd be teaching him all *she* knew, and that he'd adore it, lucky man.

Tomorrow it would be back to the murder, but for tonight they could surrender to the feelings surging inside them and, fuelled by Rose de Noir, melt beautifully into a blissful paradise, with one of Sian's extremely healthy breakfasts to await them in the morning, much to Willie's chagrin.

***

Donald Parkforth and Belinda Thredsham has been discussing the matter. A meeting tomorrow with a senior officer could mean only one thing. Their past was going to be dragged up and they were about to be plunged into the heart of a murder investigation. They'd done their time, why couldn't they be left alone? But unbeknown to them a newspaper reporter was also on their case.

Chapter Sixteen

Donald Parkforth looked very relaxed, which Sheelagh was convinced he wasn't, as he stretched out in an armchair, legs crossed nonchalantly, and nursed a cold glass of water Belinda had brought him. He wore a plain white T-shirt, pale green shorts, white socks and Adidas trainers, whereas his partner, who had provided all four of them with water, was in a long flowing brownish Kaftan with four long splits, up to the armpits, as Willie would've described them, and bare feet. Willie didn't doubt she was without underwear but there was no way of proving it.

"Listen, Chief Inspector, we've done our time. You obviously know all about us but why you think we should've had anything to do with that woman's murder I don't know. Just because we've got records, isn't it? In the end we worked hard until retirement and here we rest, our debt to society fully paid up. Now this whole bloody village is going to know. Why can't we be left in peace?"

"How much money did you lose with Wood Falcon Developments?" Sheelagh asked sharply.

"What?"

"Do you want me to repeat the question?"

"No, it was plenty. Ruined us, and we'd saved hard in the hope of landing big dividends. None of your business how much."

"I see. How well did you know Mr Wood and Mr Falcon?"

"I answered all these questions when I was thoroughly investigated at the time of Wood Falcon's collapse, and I was cleared. Entirely innocent. That's all I have to say."

"The business didn't collapse, did it? The police caught up with it."

"What does it matter, Chief Inspector? This is getting boring."

"Mrs Thredsham," Sheelagh was changing tack, "you had two cautions for assault in your youth. Maybe that's why we're interested as we're looking into a crime of violence." Belinda rolled her eyes.

84

"Oh gawd, you think I killed her. It happened years ago. I gave a couple of other girls a seeing-to cos they were asking for it. Years ago. No, I didn't kill Mrs Merde."

"And where exactly is this getting us," Douglas intervened employing his best suave George Sanders voice.

"Perhaps drugs, Mr Parkforth. Mrs Thredsham knows all about drugs."

"Yeah, done me time for that as well. My husband died of an overdose but I expect you know that. God, you're horrible, you are. The fuzz at their worst."

"You weren't supplying Mrs Merde with drugs?"

"You're joking …."

"Was she supplying you?" Sheelagh noticed the involuntary twitch and temporary look of surprise in Belinda's face. There was almost fear etched there, but the appearance swiftly vanished.

"No, no way. I'm clean. Got clean in prison. Full stop. Look, we didn't know the Merdes. He proved to be useless as a carpenter and he was sent packing. That's all there is to know."

The meeting ended soon after, the DCI feeling the issue of drugs was somehow relevant, and the detectives left, far from convinced about either of their interviewees.

***

Trevor Bargeman was back from Northumberland and he and wife Sheena were dining in the *Downsman*. He was anxious to catch up on news and Felicity Trumpling was anxious to disgorge gossip on a grand scale. Trevor and Sheena rather despised the landlady's approach, but nonetheless took on board much of what she was saying.

A tasty main course of baked Atlantic cod was devoured with pleasure and washed down with an ice-cold *San Miguel* in Trevor's case, and a white wine spritzer for Sheena. They'd wisely booked a table for the pub was thronging with lunchtime trade, drinkers and diners alike. As they sat back, their stomachs filled most enjoyably, they looked around them and saw strangers and villagers, and took in the buzz about the place, something that had once been sadly lacking immediately after the pandemic.

They could hear snippets of conversation, about the success of England's Lionesses, who had managed to do what the men hadn't and won the European Championships; about the Prime Minister's resignation and the battle to succeed him; about the looming strikes and the upcoming cost-of-living crisis; about the heatwave conditions and the threat of climate change; and, of course, about Little Scampering's murder.

Someone had made a check and there had, apparently, been no other murders in the village down the years, although, it was claimed, there had been two violent assaults in the late 19th century, and an accidental death in 1932 when a farm worker had been trampled by a cow.

No mention was made of the second world war as everyone in the pub appeared to be too young to remember, and yet the Bargemans imagined the Battle of Britain must've raged in the skies above the village. In fact, Trevor knew that a Messerschmitt had crashed nearby and the pilot captured by the home guard. They overheard nothing about the war in Ukraine. Once front page news on a daily basis it was now relegated apart from when some extreme event took place, and they felt sorrow that it was no longer at the forefront of people's minds.

They cared passionately about that, and felt for the Ukrainian folk suffering a constant hell from which there seemed to be no relief. They cared as well because they feared the war escalating.

It was Sheena's day off, and after their repast they set off at a stroll for home, Trevor in his straw boater, Sheena under a headscarf, neither head protection offering respite from the early afternoon sun beating down as usual.

"Sad really, Trevor, when you think about it, that this lovely little village, off the beaten track, quite idyllic, a place we hoped we'd enjoy our retirement in, should be such a sorrowful hamlet. I find it hard to imagine that a woman was mercilessly stabbed to death right here, and I'm not sure I want to live here anymore. We're not retired yet, we could afford a move, what do you think, darling?" He squeezed her arm gently.

"I'd been thinking along the same lines myself but didn't know how to broach it as I know you've loved it here. No, let's up sticks and find another quiet spot." She smiled so beautifully he could've fallen in love with her all over again. Then they kissed, a soft little tender kiss, and then they found they had developed a spring in their step as they headed for home.

****

A little later the village found itself the focal point of local news once more when Roger Kempson was mown down by a drink-driver who was arrested in due course. Fortunately, Poojah Nagarka was nearby and raced to the scene and probably saved Roger's life with her skills as it was some time before the paramedic arrived, to be followed by the ambulance and the police. Edith heard the noise and went out to investigate, saw what looked like a bad accident and returned indoors, whereupon Grace phoned her with the news.

It was early evening when they learned that Roger was badly hurt but recovering in hospital, and that he owed his life to the quick thinking Poojah. Villagers were very grateful but the heroine of the hour was self-effacing and wanted none of the praise that was about to be heaped on her.

Meanwhile Edith had located a cool spot indoors where a portable fan whirled and oscillated back and forth to increase her comfort, and there she studied her map and her notes.

"Dear map," she said out loud, "tell me your secrets. You are trying to tell me something important and I cannot see what it is. Why, oh why, do I think the answer is there? Please tell me." And at that point she realised she had become increasingly interested in finding the killer, acknowledging that she had been swept up by the eager Grace Cathcart, and now wanted to investigate further.

I've never liked those TV programmes, she thought, although I quite enjoyed *Foyle's War*, and I've never wanted to read a murder mystery novel, but I have to admit to being fascinated by the concept now, as if I have any chance of solving this one!

But the seeds had been sown in her mind. Who shall I be, she asked herself? Miss Marple or Hercule Poirot? What about Morse? I cannot reconcile myself to the thought of achieving popularity and fame as Footlong. I don't know, though. Edith Footlong Investigates! Sounds alright I suppose. Perhaps just Footlong, ace detective. Yes, might do the trick. Of course, I haven't been metricated yet so I should be Edith Thirty-centimetres-long!

And she laughed out loud. You fool, she silently admonished herself, and went back to her precious map, hoping some inspiration that had so far escaped her might appear before her very eyes. It was a task doomed to failure for the time being, but maybe not forever.

The following evening she was summoned to Grace's to await Sally Cainton who had news, so Edith had been told.

***

The Merde brothers were at their father's and temperatures were rising which had nothing to do with the exceptional hot weather.

Finally, Stephen could stand it no longer and openly accused his father of stabbing his beloved mother, an act that annoyed Albert beyond reason, and the two quickly came to blows while an astonished Carl looked on. He had to try and intervene. This was getting ridiculous.

He rushed across to the pair and was knocked unconscious by one of Albert's flying fists, which missed its intended target, his brother. At least that calmed the situation, if only temporarily. They carried Carl to the settee and laid him down where Albert sought a pulse and was told it was a pointless exercise as their father was still breathing. Animosity once more reared its ugly head until Stephen withdrew from the fray and went to the phone.

"Better dial, what is it, 111, and ask for help. He may need treatment." Albert conceded the point and took the remaining heat out of the situation by going for a cold flannel which, he assumed, might help their stricken father. Gradually Carl came round and seemed none the worse for his ordeal. Stephen had been advised, as it was technically a head injury, to take him to hospital, but Carl had no time for doctors, hospitals and the medical profession generally, so he refused. Albert said in no uncertain terms if he didn't feel well they would be going, full stop.

The most important outcome of this unseemly behaviour was that peace was restored between the brothers, even if it was an uneasy truce.

Chapter Seventeen

Sally Cainton had no intention of disclosing all her information and restricted herself to the bare bones and no flesh at all. Edith recognised this but Grace did not. What is she hiding, Edith wondered, as the reporter's dialogue continued? There was no doubt she'd discovered much more than she was saying but was guarding her story knowing it could be useful to any other hack after an exclusive, and she wanted to be first. These ladies might spread gossip that could reach the wrong ears, and in Grace's case that was most definitely the situation!

"It wouldn't be fair to dig up their past just for the sake of it," she argued with all the false sincerity she could manufacture, "as this could ruin the lives of innocent people. I'll be completely honest with you," she added with over-the-top earnestness, "but both Parkforth and Thredsham have been inside, admittedly a long time ago, and they were investigated over a matter of fraud more recently, and cleared. Please don't spread this around, ladies, as, assuming they are innocent of Mrs Merde's killing, they should be left in peace."

Grace gasped. Criminals in their midst! Horror of horrors. She suddenly found she couldn't remember locking her front door, and then recalled she was in her own home. Pull yourself together, woman, she remonstrated with her alarmed self, which was all for going to pieces.

Sally was feeling delighted with the results, and was confident Grace would let the cat out of the bag sooner rather than later, and hopefully embellish the tale with a few juicy additives to make matters worse.

"Please keep this under wraps for a few days while I file my article and make further enquiries. I wouldn't want another paper stealing my scoop."

Edith felt as if she was observing all this from a distance, for she was watching both Sally and Grace carefully and believed she had the former figured out for what she was, a devious manipulator.

"Tell me, ladies," Sally continued, "when there's a murder, whether it's in town or country, we normally end up writing things like '*the local community was shocked and stunned*' and explain how neighbours talked of the victim as being such a beautiful person. But here, in Little Scampering, there may have been shock initially, but life's just going on, and nobody has a good word to say about the Merdes, almost as if everyone wants Carl charged pronto so you can get back to the proverbial day job, as it were. Why is that?" Edith stepped in quickly, sensing Grace was preparing a response the length of 'War and Peace'.

"Our village has become a kind of place people move to from the urban areas. It pushes up property prices so that young local people have to move to more reasonably priced areas. Mrs Cathcart has lived here all her life as you know, and I was born here and returned when nearing retirement, so I feel I've come back home. The village hasn't developed as a close-knit community. There are many incomers, most seeking a retirement escape to the country. We have the pub, but not everybody drinks, and no other community hub. People have become friends with like-minded people but otherwise we've tended to keep ourselves to ourselves.

"The Merdes did nothing to merge in with existing villagers, and maybe we did nothing to help them feel welcome. It's the way it's been. Gossip does the rest. Carl was not a good carpenter, but I only know that from gossip, however accurate it might be. I think you'll find the answer in there somewhere, Sally. They weren't liked because they did nothing to be warm and friendly. Contrast that with how we all feel about Roger Kempson. A much loved character mown down by a drink-driver, so we're told, and we all care very much. We are indeed shocked that a murder has taken place in Little Scampering, but not very sensitive to those involved. Does that help?" Sally was just staring at her and thinking that it served her right for asking!

"Yes, I think that sums it up very succinctly, Mrs Footlong. But now this has happened, and as you obviously understand what's wrong with your village, why not try and put it right? Why not try and form, well, a residents' association and have occasional events, or even a neighbourhood watch, especially after this terrible crime?" Grace jumped straight in.

"Oh Sally, what a marvellous idea, don't you agree, Edith?" Edith gave a slight nod and left her response at that. Their visitor departed soon after content that she had planted a concept that would be developed and might be to her benefit in time to come. The village expose was still foremost in her thoughts.

"I must say, Edith, I thought you were marvellous, although I was surprised the extremes you went to in order to explain village life. I wasn't expecting something the length of 'War and Peace'. But you handled her well, and that's the important thing." Edith inhaled slowly and swallowed.

"Thank you Grace," a slightly disgruntled Edith responded, hoping her contempt was being kept from her voice, "and I think we have the acorn of an idea there. I think a residents' group would be ideal, don't you?" Edith was several steps ahead in her own planning and thinking about the investigative advantages of meeting the other villagers. Why, that would be the perfect opportunity to talk to everyone, absolutely everyone, and, at the same time, almost as an aside, ask them about their response to the murder. Clues might abound!

"Yes Edith, what a grand scheme. But could we organise something like that?"

"First of all let's go and speak to the rest of the villagers, individually, see what they think, and I've no doubt one or two 'leaders', if you get my meaning, will emerge! Some folk like to be involved in those things. We can start the movement and someone else can take over. Rest assured, someone out there will want to be head-cook-and-bottle-washer!"

***

Edith returned home and arrived just as PC Bowlman was walking past.

"How about a cold drink, officer?" she said with a smile.

"That would be so kind, and yes please, I'd love one." They went indoors and Thomas helped open the windows and the patio doors while Edith prepared their drinks. She switched on a fan and they slipped into a cool spot to enjoy the refreshments.

"Thomas, so rude of me, would you like something to eat?"

"No, no, I'm fine Mrs Footlong, but thanks."

"If you don't mind me asking, Thomas, and I know you can't talk about the case, but I was curious about the whole business. We've only learned what was in the news. You came as part of the team that arrived on the day. What can you actually tell me about that terrible tragedy?"

"Well, as far as I know, Mr Merde called the police when he found the body of his wife. That must've been indescribably awful, finding her like that, and she'd been stabbed to death on her patio. That's about it really, probably all you know anyway. There are some other aspects that I can't talk about, but I'm not on the investigation team so there's possibly much more. Sorry I can't be more helpful. Why the interest, Mrs Footlong?"

"I often take newspaper stories with a pinch of salt. They do say don't believe all you read in the papers. It's so sad, it's just so black and white and dreadful. Man finds wife murdered on their patio, and there's not much more to it than that for the onlooker."

"I know, but I'm confident we'll get to the bottom of it. Our DCI Sheelagh Mehedren, well, I've got so much faith in her and the team, I'm sure they'll crack it soon."

With that he thanked his host and set off on patrol leaving Edith to wonder how much longer his lonely vigil would last in the village that didn't care. Mmm …. she considered, that would make a good title for a book, 'The Village that didn't Care', but I expect it's been done already. It is rather like that, though, Little Scampering. Sally was quite right about the lack of reaction, the lack of concern, the lack of sensitivity, but hey-ho, most villagers had condemned poor Mr Merde out of hand. Perhaps he'll be charged soon, but then again maybe he's not the killer.

***

And it came to pass that July slipped away, almost unnoticed, a seamless transition to August that might well be just as hot as the preceding month. Another heatwave was forecast. Kent continued to swelter, most of those on holiday loved it, some couldn't stand it, and some saw their health suffer. Asthmatic Nancy Harmand was one of the latter, often struggling for breath in the stifling lack of air. Roger Kempson continued to recover in hospital and was visited there by Edith and Grace. In time the police presence in the village disappeared and Mrs Merde's funeral was held, attended by none of her neighbours, but by plenty of her family who treated it more as an excuse for a party than a solemn affair for reflection.

Grace was shocked to see the group return from the 'afterwards-at' clutching bottles and beer cans and laughing and joking. One of Albert's daughters, in a disrespectfully short black mini-dress, was standing on the pavement swigging wine straight from the bottle.

Along with Edith, Grace had started the door-to-door apropos forming a residents' group and both ladies had been pleased with the general response which was promising. But progress was later rudely interrupted by a bombshell.

***

Alison Digbin's life was at a very low ebb. Peter had made the situation all too clear that time last month and she was now reduced to the level of a Victorian servant, unable to find anything much to enjoy. However, following Edith's visit, and having discussed the matter with her, Alison's interest in gardening was rekindled with Edith promising to give her a hand from time to time. Mrs Footlong was widely regarded as a first-class gardener, not that anyone was currently enjoying much luck in the heat frying the countryside.

Water was a key problem. There was a shortage leading to a hosepipe ban, and most villagers could not understand why so many houses were being built in the county when the supply of water was such an issue.

Edith took Alison on a tour of her small but perfectly formed rear garden, which only served to rejuvenate the poor woman, and showed her the waste water diversion system which she'd devised and created. She'd sawn off the bottom of the downpipe from the bath where the pipe ran outside, and placed a water butt there to catch all the bath and shower water.

"I tend to use baby products that are clearly harmless to plants," Edith enthused to a startled Alison, "and in winter I disconnect the butt, move it away, and put a temporary tube down into the drain. Voila! I rarely use a hose anyway, and, as you can see, have three other butts connected to the rainwater downpipes. Simples, as my granddaughter says."

This new interest was a corner-stone for Mrs Digbin's recovery, and, although unbeknown to both women, the start of what was to become the Little Scampering Gardening Club.

In fact, Edith's new project was the birthplace of a number of ideas that was to unite the village, as well as providing the would-be sleuth with a range of investigative possibilities in relation to the murder. But first there was a different kind of difficulty to be overcome.

Chapter Eighteen

"Eeny, meeny, miny, mo, catch poor Willie by his toe; if he hollers let him go, eeny, meeny, miny, mo." Willie looked at his boss with as much scorn as he could summon up in the time available.

"What's that about, ma'am?"

"Do I charge Carl or not? I've taken it upstairs and they ask if we've been down every avenue, explored every possibility, and so on. They're as nervous as I am of charging on purely circumstantial evidence. There are some tough defence barristers out there, Willie. We need a breakthrough, in any blinking direction. Basically, half the village *might* have done it, but then we could be looking at an outsider, maybe someone from London. There just isn't one flipping clue, not one."

"Never mind, ma'am," soothed Willie, trying to sound sympathetic, "we all know something can come out of the blue. Perhaps we need another amateur sleuth….." Sheelagh gave him a glance that might've pierced his flesh. "Sorry, only joking."

"Hmph. You'd better be. I thought that reporter was going to get in the way but she seems to have gone quiet. So what have we got?"

"Nothing, a big zero, relating to the Merdes time in Eltham. Both grew up there, married there and had a flat for years and years. Two offspring, Albert, with his old-fashioned name, and Stephen. Carl was a carpenter, self-employed, did mainly contract work, some domestic, not a lot.

Our colleagues have talked to a couple of builders who used him in recent times, said he was okay, no problems. Also talked to neighbours, bit non-committal apparently, nothing derogatory, but perhaps the Merdes didn't hit it off up there either.

"Alana seems to have spent her married life doing as little as possible apart from raising the two boys, much as Carl explained, and was not involved, so we are told, in any local activities or anything like that.

"According to Carl her life revolved around having family and friends visit, which he was left to arrange, which often required giving out a three-line whip when necessary, so it would seem, and castigating anyone who pulled out of a visit. What a life!"

"And Willie, no obvious connection, historical or otherwise, with villagers in Little Scampering. No, Carl's my number one choice, unless he, she or they were up to their eyeballs in something shady or positively illegal. House turned upside down by forensics, likewise the garden. Nowt. Where do we go from here?" Willie, having listened intently, studied his notes in the vain hope that an answer might leap off the pages at him.

At this desperate stage neither of them realised that another amateur sleuth might be riding to their rescue soon! Memories of dealing with Ernest Pawden when seeking the killer of Gareth Modlum were still raw in their minds, as was the fact that an innocent old lady nearly lost her life thanks to their prevarication. And Sheelagh was vacillating again for want of a clue. Such indecision might once again place a lady's life in peril.

***

The lady in question, Edith Footlong, had been busy with her new dual-project: trying to get a sense of community going in the village, and using the opportunity to ask more detailed questions about the killing.

Usually she tackled the community aspect first, adding the murder as an after-thought, and by so doing encouraged people to speak. Her notebook was filling fast. As she had anticipated there were one or two eager volunteers when it came to forming a residents' group, Mr Harper in particular keenly describing how he had chaired a similar group where they lived prior to their move to the village.

It was but a simple measure to conclude her chat with the Harpers by remarking how sad it was that nobody was overly concerned about a major crime in their midst, a simple measure to employ but a productive one.

"Well," gushed Mrs Harper, "the sad truth is that nobody liked them very much. I mean, we had nothing to do with them anyway but the Sonnels next door had to live with them on their doorstep. Have you seen them yet?" Edith shook her head. "Often complained to us about the Merdes, you know, the bad language and the noise and so on. I wouldn't mind betting they were pleased to see the back of her, loud-mouthed tart. Did you ever see those tiny dresses she wore out the front?" Edith shook her head again. "She'd bend over to pull up a weed and, well, well, she'd be showing far too much for one of her advanced years." Mr Harper took up the story.

"It was disgusting, shocking. No, I agree with my wife, I don't suppose she'll be missed and quite frankly the sooner he's charged and put away the better."

"All the same," Edith began, "a gory end, stabbed on the patio, and left for the husband to find her …"

"Gory, yes, but he didn't find her, Edith, he killed her." Mr Harper's sharply spoken words had a finality about them and Edith did not tarry any longer.

It was much the same wherever she went. Even Felicity Trumpling at the pub was damning despite saying how entertaining the Merdes arguments were.

"I've got to say it, Edith, they were nice enough sober, but a couple of drinks and they were often away. I think arguing was just normal conversation for them, but it didn't endear them to the villagers, know what I mean? But a horrible way to die, and how sick was that? Having your body neatly arranged after you've been killed. Sick. Trouble is, I agree with the general opinion round here that he did it, and the sooner the police lock him up the better. I don't want to think that there might be a deranged murderer out there, because who might be next, I ask you?"

Mr Sonnel also appeared to be enthusiastic about a residents' group of some sort, and demonstrated his own credentials for management by relating all the work he had done that required his leadership. He was firmly into his stride, and Edith was feigning interest and suffering boredom, but he could not stop himself being in full flow when it came to the time for the murder to be mentioned. Poor Mrs Sonnel had made several attempts to speak, all in vain, and the situation for her didn't improve with the change of subject.

"Dreadful couple," Mr Sonnel roared, barely drawing breath after his previous discourse on his managerial success, "utterly detestable, weren't they dear?" Mrs Sonnel went to answer but was yet again cut short. "Noise, language. Not surprised he killed her on the patio since she spent most of the summer out there being waited on hand and foot. I expect he said 'that'll teach you' as he stabbed her! Evil woman, and what a lame excuse for a man. Pussy-footed around after her. We used to hear her ask him to go and get things for her that were only a few feet away on the patio itself. Lazy woman, wasn't she dear?" Mrs Sonnel failed to make any vocal impact as had been the case thus far. "He told us once, in the early days, that she was like that, a pampered princess he called her."

By the time Edith left not only were her ears worn out but Mrs Sonnel had still not got a word in edgeways. Time to go home for a cuppa, make up the notes and then call on Grace.

**

August brought with it the inevitable bombshell, and a temporary curtailment of Edith's efforts. Sally Cainton's feature on life in a quiet, rural Kentish village took everyone by surprise. It sought to lift the lid on the peaceful rustic idyll that was face of the average hamlet and expose the world that lay underneath. Her article used a fictitious name for the settlement, and all the characters had fictional names, but as a recent murder and a drink-driving casualty were mentioned, if not by name, there was no doubt that Little Scampering was the village.

To read it you might believe that these places were hotbeds for illicit love affairs, seething disputes, simmering discord and revolting prejudice, together with all the ingredients needed for crime to be brewing. Neighbours fighting with neighbours, the deliberate spreading of malicious rumours, villagers hopping in and out of each others houses for naughty purposes. It was all there. Grace and Edith's alter egos were portrayed as gossipers-in-chief, which led to Grace suffering some palpitations which Edith had to soothe.

But it had an upside, showing that good can sometimes come from evil. For the villagers became united as one overnight, making Edith's task all the easier. Letters to the paper, coming from little villages all over Kent, showed umbrage had been taken, offence given, and proclaimed that Sally's work was nonsense, absolute rubbish. The story briefly made national news but faded quite quickly.

Not everyone could cope with the situation. Donald Parkforth and Belinda Thredsham were all but destroyed by the revelations and vowed to leave the wretched place. Given the names Douglas Parland and Linda Foresham in the article they were portrayed as active criminals who might, *might* have had something to do with the murder. The feature was so obvious and so damning Mr Harper even consulted his solicitor with a view to suing the paper.

But in the end no action was taken. Perhaps strangely, the villagers drew a protective curtain around the maligned Mr Parkforth and Mrs Thredsham, and the couple found themselves in receipt of sympathy and support.

Not so Ms Towford. Given the name Susie the Floozie in the article, she eschewed offers of friendship from well-meaning people and withdrew deeper into her own cocoon. Sally had even taken a supermarket motto 'every little helps' to describe the comfort Susie could offer willing men. Edith did not give up on her, despite being rebuffed during her first call, and in time a strong bond evolved between the two.

Even Carl was swept up by this new mood and Edith was one of several villagers who came to know him better and to befriend him. After all, he still had not been charged, so maybe, just maybe he was innocent.

On one of her visits he opened up again about finding his wife. "It was dark, Edith. I wondered where she was and found the patio door open. It was a hot night and I assumed she needed some air. And there in the darkness she was." Tears filled his eyes but did not fall. "I took one look, I couldn't even go out there, I really couldn't. I saw the knife and knew she was dead. I came straight back in here and phoned. I didn't kill her Edith, I didn't." And she believed him, more than ever.

And that meant the killer was still at large.

***

The DCI was looking at the pathologist's report for the umpteenth time. Alana was five foot nine in old money, as Sheelagh termed it, the knife was old, double edged and plunged deep into the chest, horizontally, exactly horizontally. This meant, upon experiment, that the killer must've taken aim to ensure a clean, direct blow through the heart. Even in the dark Alana must've seen it coming, regardless of her being stunned by the attack, yet she appeared to have taken no avoiding action. The blow was too deliberate in the pathologist's opinion and Sheelagh was inclined to agree. So was it someone who knew exactly what they were doing? The knife would have to be raised to inflict the wound. It wasn't a sudden impulse thrust, of that she was sure.

Alana should've had a moment to scream, perhaps to take a step back, maybe even to run. Was she too shocked? There was something not quite adding up, but what was it?

***

Harry Thrack was, to use his own choice of expression, purple with apoplexy, or at least he had been when the wretched article had appeared. His character, Wurzel Thripp, had been displayed as a dim, country yokel and he did not like it, as he explained to Edith.

"Blasted woman. How dare she? We only met once and then briefly yet she writes like she's known me all my life. And she's got me all wrong." Edith smiled to herself. Many folk were making assumptions about the fictional people in the feature. True, a few were very obvious, such as the invented names for Francesca Towford and Donald Parkforth, but most were not, yet villagers saw themselves in these pictures, as Grace had done.

"If she ever sets foot in here again there'll be another murder done in Little Scampering, so help me God." Mmmm … thought Edith … a chance to talk about Alana's demise.

"Do you think Carl Merde did it, Harry?"

"Of course. Who else? That's another thing about that blasted paper. Because the police haven't charged him we're all thinking there's a killer on the loose, and they're living right alongside us!

101

What about the police, I ask you? They're the dim country yokels in all this."

"I'm quite intrigued by the fact it was the middle of the night," Edith interrupted, keen to avoid the conversation heading in the wrong direction, "and Mrs Merde was lured out onto the patio, by her husband if you are correct, and brutally stabbed. That's horribly pre-meditated. Surely he couldn't have hated her that much?"

"I don't know so much. Maybe they had a row, like they used to have in the pub, and he just exploded, grabbed a knife from the kitchen and went for her. Alright, I don't know the man, don't really know how he felt about her, but the police haven't pinned it on anyone else, have they? Got to be him."

"What about you, Lizzie?" Edith asked Harry's wife. In a refreshing change from what she'd experienced elsewhere, Harry sat back quietly and the let Lizzie say her piece, never once looking as if he would interrupt. A gentleman, not a yokel by any means, Edith decided.

"I don't know. I think the police know much more than they're telling us, and are probably more advanced in their investigations that we realise. It doesn't do to tell all and sundry what they're up to. I wouldn't be surprised if they don't suddenly make an arrest and shock us all. Long as it's not Harry!" And they all laughed. "No Edith, I'm not certain about Mr Merde, but then I'm not certain the killer is lurking in our midst."

The next stop was Mr and Mrs Burns at Len View House. An interesting name for a small cottage from which there was absolutely no view of the river Len, nor any real view of the valley. Luke Burns had owned a restaurant of some renown that was virtually killed off by the pandemic, but he was able to sell the premises and retire about six months earlier than he should've done. His wife, Eileen, had finished an extraordinarily varied career as an assistant at a veterinary practice. A former secretary, a council worker, doctor's receptionist, farm worker, parking warden and, of course, mother, had all been part of a remarkable story. They'd had five children, all now had their own marriages and careers, and had presented their parents with, so far, fourteen grandchildren.

In the paper their 'typically cute, cramped little cottage' had been called 'Ben View House' and the couple named as 'Len and Irene Berry' but both refused to acknowledge these aspects were anything other than products of a writer's vivid imagination.

"Come in, Mrs Footlong, come in."

"Thank you, Mr Burns, and please call me Edith."

"Thank you, Edith, and we're Luke and Eileen."

"Come and sit down in here, Edith," Eileen suggested as she led the way into the lounge, "please sit where you like. We're delighted you've come and so pleased you've taken up the gauntlet to bring a sense of community to our disparate villagers, especially after that rubbishy newspaper story and the murder, of course." Perfect; straight into their visitor's second phase!

"Oh wasn't that paper business awful? But I do think some of our neighbours have made the assumption the fictional characters are them. If the cap fits, of course ...." A merry little chuckle fell upon them and decorated the room. "Sadly, a few have been made *very* obvious and I feel so sorry for them, but I understand from our phone call you do not consider yourselves among them."

"No, of course not," Eileen replied, producing another little chuckle which she generously passed on to her husband, both smiling quite cheerily.

"But the murder was frightful. I think the police are doing much better than they're letting everyone know, and I'm sure they'll make an arrest very soon. What do you think?" This open-ended invitation lured out the required response, Luke stepping smartly to the fore.

"Yes, but I, well, that is, both of us, feel Mr Merde is the most likely person, don't you? We think that he was alone with her and there doesn't seem to be anything to suggest anyone else was there, and he simply stabbed her, whether it was in a rage or he'd just had enough. There have been so many rumours and we don't like gossip ...."

"That's right, dear. Luke is right, we think gossip is detestable, and often so bad for the people involved, particularly if they are innocent. So no, we 're not convinced it was Mr Merde, but then we're at a loss at to which villager might have committed such a heinous crime. Perhaps it was someone from elsewhere, what do you think, Edith?"

"I'm keeping an open mind, naturally, but I suppose I really don't want to think that Mr Merde or anyone from the village did it."

"Assuming he didn't," Luke added, "it would've been an unimaginable shock to come upon your wife like that." The three of them sat in silence for a moment or two reflecting on the distress that must've overtaken Carl Merde in that horrific situation.

There wasn't much more to discuss on the subject and Edith left shortly after, having ascertained their wholehearted support for a united Little Scampering.

***

"Now, who's on strike today, Edith?" Grace was looking baffled as she poured some apple juice for the pair of them, a preferred refreshment to hot beverages on these scorching days, and settled back in her favourite armchair located in a relatively cool spot, chilled by a small portable fan.

"I don't know, Grace. I can't keep up! Still, never mind, at least we pensioners are not on strike, although what we would achieve by pursuing such a course of action, well, heaven knows." Their main topic of conversation today was their community project, and with it their plans for the future of Little Scampering.

"Most have been quite keen, Grace, two or three showing marked enthusiasm, and, as predicted, leaders are emerging! I also believe animosity towards Carl may be softening although there is a core who have him on the gallows, in a manner of speaking. There seems to be a greater feeling that, if he is innocent, he should be pitied, and that his guilt is not a foregone conclusion at present. The times they are a-changing, Grace."

Later, back home, Edith wrote up her latest notes in the usual meticulous fashion, and tried to cross-reference, but the heat and lack of air was oppressive, and she could not concentrate. Instead she resorted to making a salad sandwich which she enjoyed on a sheltered part of her own patio while listening to some gentle background music on a CD.

I'll get sorted tomorrow, she told herself. Indeed, she would.

Chapter Nineteen

Outside the pub Eric Trumpling was standing in a yellow-ish-brown patch once known as a lawn and scratching his head. To Edith's fertile mind he took on the appearance of a man who had a beautiful lawn last night and had suddenly found it barren this morning. Of course, the sun had been working on it for days and days and days for it to reach its present condition, as Eric well knew.

"Don't worry, Eric," Edith called out as she approached, "it'll come back once it rains."

"Aye, I know that love, but the sceptic in me can't quite believe it," he chuckled as he turned to face the ladies. Edith and Grace were out soon after dawn to take a healthy walk before the heat rendered such exercise undesirable.

"Gather business is good these days, Eric. You did very well indeed riding out the pandemic."

"Yes, it was hard work but well worth it. I really had to rely on the missus, y'know, but she proved herself to be one in a million, one in a million."

"Lovely to hear you say that Eric," Grace chipped in.

"I'm not ashamed to admit she was the driving force behind me. What a woman! You know, I can never understand men who stray, she's my everything, why look for something more?"

"A very refreshing way of looking at enduring love, Eric," Grace said admiringly.

"Aye. Besides, Felicity's told me exactly what she'd do to me and my lover if I ever strayed!"

The three shared a hearty chortle, but Edith thought she recognised a coldness in Eric's attitude at that point, and began to wonder if his wife had in fact explained in excruciating detail how he'd suffer if he stepped out of line in that respect. Perhaps he wasn't joking!

"Anyway, should be mowing this lawn, so I'll have to find something else to do!"

They bid their farewells and the ladies continued on their walk, up and along one of the many footpaths around this part of the Kent Downs, chatting about this and that, Grace still trying to find out who was on strike. Then she changed the subject dramatically.

"Just thinking about Eric. That sounds like real abiding love to me. He speaks so well of Felicity, and I know he was only joking in a typically masculine sort of way, but I wondered why he said that about her, you know, about her warning him. I don't suppose she ever has as I'm sure she thinks the world of him. But he's right; why do men need to stray?" Edith digested all of this carefully before replying.

"It's not just men, Grace, I'm afraid it's women too. Of course he was only joking about Felicity taking him to task; take no notice, my dear. I don't know why some people cannot be faithful. Maybe it's in their genes, I don't know. Happily we both found true and lasting happiness with the best of men, and now we can enjoy true friendship with each other." Grace hugged her arm and smiled with great contentment.

"Oh Edith, that's such a lovely thing to say, it really is. Thank you. Bless you." And they continued their walk in even better spirits.

***

The laughably named 'social' media had flared into unpleasant action after Sally Cainton's expose was published and for a brief while glowed red hot with aggression towards the author and the paper, while there was mocking counter-comment from townies rubbishing the country folk. A nasty business. But one post in particular came to Sally's attention. It read:

'You ruined my life. Now I'll finish yours. I'm good at that'

Several posts had slipped into the realms of being threatening, but this one sent a shiver down Sally's spine. It was so simple, so direct. The last line 'I'm good at that' had a special resonance for the reporter. Was it written by someone who had settled a score in the past with extreme violence? And that line of thinking took her to the murder of Alana Merde. Three people in particular sprang to mind, three people who might well bear a grudge against Sally, three people who, she knew, loathed her for exposing them. Douglas Parkforth, Belinda Thredsham and Francesca Towford. All, she was aware, had found life unbearable after her article went to press, not that it bothered a ruthless writer like Sally.

Douglas and Belinda had criminal records, Belinda a history of violence. Surely their neighbours in Little Scampering had a right to know who was living amongst them? Francesca had written to the paper to complain. Her private life had effectively been set out in public, she might be forced to move, it was a disgusting way to ruin an innocent person's life. The editor had responded by pointing out both village and occupants in the feature were fictitious. She couldn't possibly have seen herself thus portrayed?

Sally considered Francesca's letter. She'd said her life had been ruined, and that was a similar aspect of the social media post. No time to lose. She'd contact the police.

***

Sheelagh Mehedren stared at Willie Broughton who stared back at the DCI.

"Right, tell me I'm not hearing this, Willie. This daft woman writes a defamatory story about Little Scampering in disguise, maligns the residents and then wants us to protect her from angry responses." Willie had taken the call from Sally and had enlightened the DCI as to the contents. "I don't know, this sort of thing just winds me up. What did she expect? Letters of congratulations, bouquets of flowers, adoring messages of support? Log it, tell her you've spoken to me, and we'll get back to her. Probably in two years time, but don't tell her that!"

"Should we take it a bit seriously, ma'am? We're still no nearer finding Alana's killer."

"Take yer point, Willie. Okay, send Sian to see Ms Towford. She can sum up the situation, Francesca's reaction and all that, and issue a veiled warning, maybe. Don't know about the other two. They do have records, unfortunately, but how close dare we go to 'police harassment'? Let me think about them."

***

Life was improving for Alison Digbin. She did as she was told, made sure she didn't ruffle her husband's feathers, remained in the background and discovered a kind of contentment. Her meeting with Edith had given her hope. Indeed, the woman was just the inspiration she needed, suggesting she would help with the gardening, especially when summer eventually came to an end, and could be a good friend.

Peter was leaving her alone, that is, not beating her, and she was more relaxed than she'd been in a long while. She was still concerned about Carl, or more importantly, Carl betraying her, but she needn't have worried. If anything, he was quite protective of the woman who'd shown him kindness he wasn't accustomed to, and he'd never betray her to her husband. Peter had read but ignored Sally's work, and there had been no repercussions.

But how she wished the police would catch the killer so that Little Scampering could return to the proverbial shadows, out of the public gaze.

***

The relationship between the Pilchards was also improving. It may be that recent events in the village, to say nothing of Sally's essay, and Edith's visit regarding future community development, had provided some sort of basis for reconciliation and revival, but whatever it was this couple were now back to being very close and loving. Kathy wanted it all to get better, knew it would take time, and accepted that her husband was truly contrite and wished it to work.

Forgiveness had come. She wouldn't forget, and he realised that, but both were hoping they could build on this fresh beginning, and were willing to try.

The Bargemans had been studying *Rightmove* online in their quest for a new abode away from this unfortunate little settlement. At first it had been fun, as they searched around the places they knew they loved and wouldn't mind moving to, but after a while it began to pall and they wondered if they really wanted to go.

"Could be swapping old nick for the devil," Trevor advised.

"Then there's all the trouble moving, you know, dealing with the agents, solicitors and so on, and it all takes time and bother," Sheena added.

"And there's all the packing up to do, unpacking when we get there….."

"And we might not find exactly what we're looking for…."

"And Edith Footlong has come up with a good idea for uniting the village…" They paused and looked at each other then burst into laughter and grabbed each other for a cuddle. Trevor continued:

"Okay, it's on the proverbial back burner, Sheena. Now, what's for tea, darling?" And they laughed some more.

***

DC Sian Stramer rang to make an appointment with Francesca who wasn't at all pleased about it, especially when Sian refused to be drawn on the purpose of her call. Ms Towford was blunt and rude and aggressive but gave in having been warned that it was an official enquiry and the police were coming anyway.

Sian gained admittance, was shown into the kitchen and offered a seat at the breakfast bar, but not offered refreshments. She explained why she was there. Francesca spoke at once.

"Right, yes, it's me, or at least I got a friend to post it. There, I've admitted it. Do I have to say it's a fair cop as you snap the cuffs on me? I confess. I wanted to frighten her and I obviously have done. It's not against the law being an escort but I live here and I didn't want anyone to know. Now she's blown my cover, to use an expression, and I feel uncomfortable so I may have to move from my lovely home here in the countryside. How would you feel, Constable? So what happens now? Do I go to court facing years in prison?" And Francesca sat down with a thump, buried her face in her hands, and then cried out at the top of her voice, "Somebody please help me."

The DC believed the distress was genuine and wanted to move and put an arm around her, but somehow knew it wouldn't help, it wasn't the sort of help she'd cried out for. So she settled for a short statement.

"I am truly sorry. No action's being taken against you. Let the matter rest. But please understand the atmosphere is very volatile and others have been snared in much the same way, so posting that item ... well ... not very smart thinking. Goodbye, Ms Towford."

As she was shown the door, neither woman speaking, they were confronted by Edith approaching up the garden path.

"Oh, Ms Towford, sorry, didn't know you had company."

"The officer is leaving. Come in Mrs Footlong. Could do with better company." Her sneering contempt was manifest in her words and facial expression, and was followed up by a rude gesture behind Sian's back as she set off. Edith overlooked it, and slipped indoors, a rather more welcome guest than when she'd first called.

***

There was no change in the weather, but one piece of good news arrived. Roger Kempson was back from hospital, much recovered, and was immediately set upon by well-meaning neighbours only too keen to do his every bidding. And he lapped it up. People are so kind, he mused with pleasure. Among the welcome visitors was his saviour, Poojah, and her husband Deepak. Very self-effacing, Poojah gently waved away the accolades, and smiled sweetly at those who praised her, saying it was nothing, just doing her job. The pair were among the few who came out of Sally's piece with any credit, and then Sally hadn't been able to resist a dig at the 'evils of British colonialism' even hinting the Nagarkas had been made to feel inferior on moving to the village.

This disgraceful slur had been shown up for the deliberate mischief making it was, Deepak making it quite clear they had been made to feel like 'one of the family'. Poojah saving Roger's life had merely added to the impression that the couple were loved in this rural location.

They had also taken excitedly to Edith's ideas, believing that a good community spirit was central to a good life well lived, Poojah even offering 'secretarial' services.

"If we all help each other we will find great contentment and a sense of well-being, and the village will thrive and be all the better for it," she'd advised, knowledgeably.

Despite the heat it had been a good year for roses. There had been some splendid blooms in gardens throughout Little Scampering, Deepak treasuring the eight he had planted and tended in his front garden, and he was very keen on the idea of a gardening club where ideas could be exchanged and assistance offered.

Edith felt it was all coming together, and that Sally's infamous work had merely served to unite them into a closer neighbourhood. Of course, she had her other project and that, like the roses, was soon to bloom.

Chapter Twenty

"Have you got time for a chat?" Francesca asked Edith, rather bluntly.

"Yes, all the time you need," came the swift response. Edith was taken into the lounge and, unlike Sian Stramer, was offered a drink, which she politely refused.

"Look, everyone knows, so I'll say what I've got to say, okay?" Edith nodded, not sure what was coming next. "I work part-time in a supermarket but I also work as an escort. You know what that is?" Edith nodded. "I don't do incalls here, I visit clients in their homes or at hotels. I don't make a nuisance of myself here. What I do shouldn't affect my life in Little Scampering, should it? You may not approve of me being an escort, but it's the oldest profession, isn't it? And I'm not interfering with people here. My work doesn't lower the value of property or anything. For God's sake. I love my home and I love, or thought I loved, Little Scampering, but I may have to move, and all because of that bloody woman, that so-called reporter. So what do I do? You tell me." And she put her head on one side and propped it up with her wrist, looking thoroughly despondent.

"You don't let Sally win. You don't move," Edith responded with strength of purpose. "So everyone knows, do they? It doesn't matter, not one jot. We're re-born. Be part of this new beginning, Ms Towford, be part of our resurrection. The police will solve the murder and then we can all move on."

"It's Francesca. Francesca if you please."

"And I'm Edith. Let's go forward together as a united village. One or two people will despise you but you'll get that wherever you go. We all know; move somewhere else and you've got to cover your tracks. Is it worth it? You've got your dream cottage and this village is going to be one damn good place to live. Come and join us."

Francesca had gradually eased her position on her armchair as she listened to Edith, who was speaking with more confidence than she felt, and was now looking wide-eyed at her visitor.

113

"Yes. Yes, I will. I won't be defeated by this, Edith. I shall win. Thank you, thank you for your words. I know you've been busy trying to get this village together and you can count on me. I don't want to move, of course I don't, and if I'm accepted as I am everyone can count me in."

Much to her surprise Edith had added another convert.

***

The DCI looked at DC Sian Stramer with eyes that unnerved the young detective.

"I see. Well, that sorts that one out, I suppose." Sian relaxed. "No need to pursue the other two now we know the identity of the perpetrator. I'll get DS Broughton to call Sally Cainton and put her mind at rest. Thanks Sian."

Sheelagh looked forlornly at the display boards in the incident room as Sian departed. We're no nearer, she thought, and it looks as if we're going to have to charge Carl. But she had no idea Edith Footlong was about to enter the fray and open up new routes.

***

Edith was partaking of cooling refreshments with Grace Cathcart, who still had no idea who was on strike.

"I'm not going to say more, dear Grace, but I think I know who the killer was. No, don't ask. I need to explore and obtain confirmation of my ideas. I will ring that DCI Mehedren that Thomas recommended and put my theories forward. I am certain the police will take me seriously and pursue my information."

Grace was stunned.

"My dear Edith, you really think you know? Good grief! But why won't you share your information with me?"

"Because I may be very wrong. After all, I've never done anything like this before. Knowing how gossip travels it could be that I am barking up the wrong tree, and my culprit may have simply heard something from someone else, perhaps the real killer. I wouldn't want to set the police on an innocent person, Grace."

114

"Well, you be careful, dear. I think the police can be very funny about being given misleading information, and you may find yourself in trouble with the law. You could be said to be wasting their time and I think that's an offence."

"Precisely, and that's why more research is needed, hence the need to keep mum, Grace." Grace was very disappointed but reluctantly accepted her friend's explanation, privately upset she was on the outside looking in when both ladies had embarked on this mission together.

***

The real killer looked out from an upstairs window admiring the pleasant view of the fields stretching away, and the many trees of so many different kinds that bounded those fields swaying slightly in the softest of breezes.

Home and dry, the killer thought. With any luck Carl will be charged and then we can all breathe a sigh of relief. There's no sign that the police can find any sort of link to me, or indeed to anyone else, and I think I'm in the clear. Nobody suspects me, not even that nosey reporter.

A crime of passion, I suppose you could say, although I was as cool as a cucumber at the time. I blazed with rage at first, but once I'd planned my revenge, right down to the final detail, the storm had passed and I was controlled, hell bent on vengeance. And I had to make sure Carl would be chief suspect and that I left no clues to me whatsoever. Clever planning!

My own doctor showed me exactly where the heart is and she never thought she was helping me with a murder! Love it, love it. Still, with any luck I'll have rid this village of the two of them, and my fellow villagers should be grateful. Just want Carl charged, then we can all be happy.

I do like Edith's ideas for regenerating Little Scampering and I'd like to be part of that. If only I could do something about this damned heat. People are just not listening to the warnings about climate change.

***

115

DC Hassana Achebe was enjoying a day off and spending lunchtime with a friend, Marie Kingley. They were sitting under a sunshade outside a country pub, far from Little Scampering, enjoying sandwiches and drinks and simply relaxing. Marie worked for an insurance firm and was based in Canterbury. They'd gone to senior school together and remained close mates having gone their separate ways career-wise. Normally they didn't touch on work but today Marie couldn't resist.

"Bad business that, Hassana. Know you can't talk about the case, but how does it affect you, you know, dealing with a murder?"

"Not good, but if I want to get on in my job I have to accept that people are capable of terrible things. I just want criminals brought to justice, like, which is why I joined, and I have to come to terms with the results of evil human behaviour. It's no good thinking oh-my-God I can't cope, you just have to. Right now we have to bring a murderer to justice, that's the most important consideration, but I approve of the way we now have specialist officers who can step in and help victims of crime. I'd like to get involved in that myself, and maybe I will in time. It's the personal touch, you know, like being there for someone. Does that make sense?"

"Definitely. Very good sense, and it's great you might want to do that. Caring people, just not enough of them in today's madcap world."

"You're not kidding. There's some real thoughtless bastards out there. Look at all the scamming that goes on online. Ruthless, disastrous for many victims. They talk about mental health issues, God, losing all your money like that is enough to make anyone ill."

"I know. Then there's all this knife crime, Hassana. I don't envy you your task at all."

"Knives are pulled for any reason these days, Marie, but quite often drugs are at the heart of it and that's where we're constantly aiming."

"Could drugs play any part in the murder you're investigating? Oh sorry, know you can't say."

"That's alright, Marie. In fact, it's a possibility these days in so many crimes. I do so wish I could discuss this one with you, I

116

really do, and I'd love to. Would like your input, but there you go." Having seemingly exhausted the subject of crime they moved on to talk about forthcoming holiday plans, and an autumn trip they were hoping to take together to Madeira.

Hassana went home later wishing that she could indeed talk about the murder with Marie. It's alright having professionals talking to victims, but *we* need someone to talk to sometimes! I know, I'll have a chat with Lucy Panshaw tomorrow. She's approachable.

***

DS Willie Broughton was, as was his custom these days, perusing his notes very thoroughly and, like his boss, hoping a clue might spring up from the pages in front of him. The DCI had taken her notes home last night to study in relative peace and quiet, undisturbed by anything at all. Frustratingly, neither officer was coming to any conclusion. Fellow Sergeant, Lucy Panshaw, was watching him as the lines furrowed deeper on his forehead.

"Willie, you'll screw your poor face up into a ball. Can I make a suggestion?" After a moment or two of resigned hesitation he looked up and nodded. "You know what? We're all too close to this. I mean, we're so on top of it that maybe we're ignoring the obvious. Oh gawd, not explaining this very well. What I mean is we need someone who is detached from the investigation to study our work. It needs to be seen from outside, if you get my drift." Willie stopped giving the impression he was chewing his tongue, went to answer, changed his mind, chewed his tongue a bit more, then spoke.

"No, Lucy, you explained it well, and I know what you mean. Ordinarily, I'd agree, but I think the complexity is the stumbling point."

"No it isn't. It isn't complex at all. Alana stabbed, all the evidence points to Carl. There's just no evidence that isn't circumstantial. If not Carl then my money's on an outsider, perhaps an intruder, who knows? Seriously, do any of the villagers look like potential killers? Of course they don't."

117

"Sadly, I know you're right, Lucy. The fact that we're sitting here, nobody is out questioning anyone, nothing is happening, all points to a dead end, if you'll pardon my expression. I think I'll give my old mate, Ernest Pawden, a ring. See if he's busy at the mo ...." Lucy was sniggering.

"Don't tell the boss, she'll have kittens! Mind you, joking all on one side, he did get the widow to open up, which is more than we did, and what was that expression he came up with?"

"Oh yes, cherchez la femme – look for the woman. Wonder what he'd say this time? Thank God we don't have to rely on amateur detectives. I don't think I could stomach another one!"

Unfortunately for Willie another one was just around the corner.

And that was without some additional and unhelpful input from Sally Cainton.

Chapter Twenty One

Grace had popped in to see Nancy Harmand who was suffering with her asthma in the intense heat. Unfortunately, in her eagerness, Grace could not help but reveal that Edith thought she knew who the killer was, but was making some final checks. Nancy could not have been less interested at that time as she was sitting in the shade desperately trying to breathe and stay alive. Her visitor tried to comfort her but there was so little she could do.

Eventually Grace simply sat in silence and watched as Nancy closed her eyes and gasped with each breath. Little tears rolled down Grace's cheeks, she couldn't stop them, and pain filled her very being. If only she could help. But the heat was intolerable and she knew her host would have to bear the worst of it, and she prayed she'd be spared and allowed to survive.

Later, she made her way to Edith's full of sadness and despair. She happened to pass Ken Waghorn and mentioned Nancy's plight to him.

"I'll call in, Grace, and just say hello, but I don't think I'm very welcome anywhere much at the moment."

"You've got that all wrong, Ken. We're reborn, Edith tells me. Go and see Nancy. I think it's important we keep a watchful eye on her in her condition. Yes, she has her inhalers and sprays, but she's losing the will to live. Let's not have another death. If she has an asthma attack at least someone can dial 999 if there's someone there with her."

Ken gave the matter great thought and in the end decided Grace was right.

"Yes, just wish this murder could be cleared up and we can all get on with life."

"Well, don't mention this to anyone Ken, but I think Edith's got the answer. She hasn't revealed all to me yet as she needs to tie up some loose ends, but I expect her to contact the police shortly."

Grace's idea of 'keeping mum' was well short of the description Edith was relying on, and, inadvertently, it would ultimately put Edith in the killer's sights.

***

The trend for dog ownership, which had blossomed during the pandemic, had spread to Little Scampering. As elsewhere, the choice of dog, or dogs, wasn't always entirely governed by the owner's needs and had to be an animal that could be shown off and, if possible, trump a neighbour's.

The Cassocks had a pair of Siberian Huskies called Minty and Sage which were often seen being bundled into the Range Rover to be taken for exercise although, in fairness, the Cassocks had a large rear garden the hounds could play in. They were also walked through the village periodically, attached to expensive looking leads and harnesses, Mr Cassock in particular bolt upright and proud, accepting the looks of admirers and creating envy in others.

The Simpsons had a lovely Weimaraner that for mysterious and undisclosed reasons was called Elleray. Grace Cathcart reckoned it was so that when the dog was summoned people would be impressed by its unusual name.

The Dumbolds had a pair of Cairn Terriers named Puskas and Putney, the former being a famous footballer in days gone by, the latter being where the Dumbolds had moved from. Edith reasoned they were lucky not to have chosen Messi and Pratt's Bottom by the same token.

Philip Plusmith had a boxer with the wholly original name of Fido, and Angela Compton possessed an aging corgi called Jilly. This one had been around for a long, long time and predated the general dog ownership surge.

One of these many hounds was destined to save Edith's life.

***

Sally Cainton wrote a follow-up feature to her original story which determined to show the police in a bad light. In it she claimed that she'd almost certainly identified the killer, meaning, of course, Francesca Towford, not that her name was mentioned in this article, but the police had dismissed her findings. All it did was alert the real killer to the concept that Sally represented a danger.

As if that wasn't bad enough the rumour had reached the murderer that Edith Footlong was also on the verge of revealing the identity of the assassin. Dealing with Edith was going to be a piece of cake, but Sally? That was going to be a tricky one.

If truth be told the purpose of Sally's discourse was principally to knock the force that she felt had shown a distinct lack of interest in the anonymous threat. From her point of view she remained in ignorance of a threat to her life. She was a woman of great self-confidence and self-belief. She would not have realised the killer was, even now, assessing how to eliminate her.

***

By now most villagers accepted the villain was not one of them, and were easily tempted to support Sally's despatch that the police weren't up to much. Carl hadn't been charged so the general opinion seemed to be that he couldn't have slain his wife after all, and attitudes started to soften towards him. It had to be an outsider and presumably the police were at a loss. There were doubts about the malefactor's identity, of course, but by-and-large they hoped the law was closer to solving this one than they were saying.

Another warning had been issued for a heatwave and the county braced itself. Indeed, the weather was now the main topic of conversation in the *Downsman,* but Edith's idea for a united village came a close second, with Roger Kempson's recovery not far behind, and talk of the murder relegated to a minimal passing subject, if mentioned at all.

Business was still brisk with plenty of folk keen to slake their thirsts with cold drinks of all kinds. Hot meals were still selling briskly but the emphasis of the food side of things was more for salads, sandwiches and snacks. They all made money for the Trumplings.

The Priors, next door to Carl, were looking forward to him either being charged and removed from their midst, or the culprit caught and the possibility Carl might want to move. The family could not do anything quietly. They slammed doors as a matter of course, talked in loud voices and argued amongst themselves. Today Stephen's wife Zoe was down along with her young daughter Myra and while the girl shut herself away, gaming on her device, Carl and Zoe found many ways to get on each others nerves.

Zoe had been angry and had been shouting, but not at either Carl or Myra.

"Shocking," Wally Prior observed, "She's the only woman I know who can have an argument with an Alexa! One day, my dear, we may be free of all this." And he returned to his newspaper while swinging slowly on the hammock which was out of the sun just down the garden, yet close enough for them to bear witness to any discord next door.

"Can't come soon enough," Beryl replied with a sigh, "because there are times when I feel I've had quite sufficient to last a lifetime!"

***

Grace was looking out of her front window and caught sight of Harry Thrack's teenage daughter walking by. My, my, she thought, I do believe that girl's forgotten to put her skirt on! And listen to her, talking into that infernal contraption, loud as you like, and so many awful words, dear me. What a world we've made for ourselves. I'm pleased I won't be around to see the dreadful consequences of all this. I wouldn't have dreamed of going out in such a short skirt, let alone using bad language at all, never mind in public. Sad times indeed.

"Now," she said to herself, "I wonder who's on strike today?"

Not far away Edith was making a lemon meringue pie which she wanted to enjoy with ice cream and single cream, and which was large enough for Grace to have a portion. She loved cooking and baking, but this wasn't the weather for extravagance in the culinary field, so this dish was a special treat, one best tasted cold. Um, she thought, a dish best tasted cold, rather like revenge if I

122

remember rightly. And do you know, if I was looking for a motive, I would say Alana Merde's death was an act of revenge. The more I think about it the more I'm convinced.

I don't think any other motive existed, that's my view. If that's the case then my guilty party, assuming I've nailed the killer, if that's the right expression, was seeking revenge for what exactly? It all points to infidelity, in my book, so was this to do with an affair Alana was having, or was it to do with Carl?

And as soon as the pie was in the oven she wrote more copious notes relating to the revenge aspect, and gradually it all became clear.

"Good," she announced loudly, "I think I'm in a position to contact the police."

***

The Sonnels had been spared the noise the Priors had been in receipt of as they were visiting family in Whitstable, but they suffered another nuisance instead.

Robert Sonnel preferred the country lanes but driving on these in Kent had become a lottery. Many lanes were closed. Water main work was often at the heart of these closures as an old creaking network was constantly springing leaks, small and large alike. Gas and electric were chipping in, and then there were closures where a new housing development was being built. It all made for a frustrating time for locals and visitors, especially when conflicting diversion signs were erected.

They'd come upon one junction where two yellow diversion boards were pointing in opposite directions, obviously relating to two separate closures, but which was which? Fortunately, Robert knew the lanes inside out and, apart from gentle cursing from time to time, was able to navigate his own way around obstructions. Who needs satnav, he'd said to Christine.

Back home late afternoon they'd slipped into the bedroom, opened the windows, put on the Dyson air filter, removed their outer clothes, and were basking in the cool air flow and the freshness that surrounded them. As they lay quietly on the bed Christine spoke.

"Do you think Carl will move back to London, Robert?"

"Shouldn't be surprised. What worries me is that, if he's innocent, and that seems to be the way things are going, he had the most almighty shock that night. I can't begin to imagine how I'd feel coming upon you like that."

"Crumbs! That sent a shiver down my spine, do you mind!"

"Sorry. But it's as unthinkable as the murder itself. And we've all treated him badly, haven't we? I think if he's not charged it'll trouble my conscience for some time to come. Alright, an obnoxious couple, but there's no excuse for poor behaviour on our part."

"Trust you, Robert. All very proper. Doing the right thing. And that's why I've always loved you." They snuggled up together, kissed, and contemplated the happiest of marriages.

"If you don't mind, Chris, I might pop round and see him …"

"I knew you were going to say that, and no, I don't mind at all. The right thing to do, eh?" And they kissed some more.

Chapter Twenty Two

Nobody on earth could've imagined it. Nobody else on earth could've experienced it. Nobody could've understood, in any way comprehended, the horrible morass of thoughts tumbling through Sheelagh Mehedren's mind on hearing Willie Broughton's words.

So few words, so much devastation. There was silence in the DCI's office, a prolonged silence while Willie considered the possibility he might need to call an ambulance, if not for the DCI then for him when she'd finished him off. Finally, she spoke. Her facial expression had not changed, she hadn't batted an eyelid, her lips hadn't moved.

"Willie," she purred, delicately and in a quiet lady-like fashion, "would you like to run that past me again?" The truthful answer was, of course, no he wouldn't because he valued his life and treasured all the parts she might play merry hell with. Instead, he cleared his throat and looked down at his notes.

"Ahem. We've had a phone call from a Mrs Edith Footlong at Little Scampering. She says she's interviewed, her word not mine, almost everyone in the village and has been able to deduce who killed Mrs Merde, and probably why. She doesn't want to discuss it over the phone and asks if we can send an officer round. Apparently, PC Bowlman told her you were leading the team and said he had every faith in you as a senior officer he admired greatly. He said, and I quote, 'I am sure the DCI will solve this case' thus reassuring Mrs Footlong. The lady therefore believes you are the right person to approach. Ma'am."

"Willie," she continued purring, "when I said run that past me again I didn't actually mean it. Why did God make men so stupid? Please tell me," she simpered, "why I shouldn't boil your head in front of the entire team?"

"Erm … sorry ma'am. Sorry."

"I heard quite clearly the first time. *Another* amateur sleuth. Just how many are there in Kent? Surely we, the police, could pack up and go home knowing the county's in safe hands. First Ernest Pawden and now Mrs Footloose …."

"Footlong, ma'am."

"Don't correct me when I'm being deliberately facetious. Okay, you can breathe out now, Willie. I am only toying with you." Willie wasn't quite convinced he liked the idea of the DCI toying with him in any way, shape or form, but he relaxed as instructed.

"And we owe this intrusion, in part, to PC Bowlman, do we? Good, send PC Bowlman to take her statement, thank him on his return, and file his report under F and F."

"F and F ma'am?"

"File and forget. Where you filed Sally Cainton's problem."

"Cool."

"Say that once more, Sergeant, and I shall hold lighted matches under your fingernails." Both officers laughed, relief at last, and Willie set off to find Thomas Bowlman.

***

Ken Waghorn had been welcomed at Nancy's and in fact spent the afternoon there. She appeared quite cheered by his visit and they indulged in wide-ranging conversation from time to time. But he could see she was struggling with her breathing and he occasionally let her rest. There was no doubt in his mind that she was enjoying his company and that it was helping her situation, and for her part she was delighted Ken was prepared to stay and entertain her.

He said he'd pop back during the evening, if that was okay, just to make sure she was alright, and she leaped at the suggestion, thanking him warmly for his concern and consideration. He returned home with a smile on his face and a spring in his step. Nancy settled down for a sleep, the happiest of ladies, and passed into the arms of Morpheus in a state of absolute contentment.

The evening's visit was even more enjoyable than the afternoon's, for Nancy was recovering as the heat subsided, and conversation was thus more jovial and pleasant. The murder wasn't mentioned once, but Edith's work at engaging a better community spirit was. Ken and Nancy were agreed it was just what Little Scampering required.

126

It was past eleven that Ken departed the second time and on this occasion he risked a little peck on his host's forehead, a gesture that was as welcome as the tenderness he'd shown throughout. He said he'd call back during the morning which filled Nancy's heart with glee. They both went to sleep that night with the most pleasurable and exciting of thoughts running through their minds.

***

Police Constable Thomas Henry Disraeli Bowlman was chuffed. He was as proud as a peacock. He checked his appearance in the car mirror several times, much to PC Emily Coombes amusement. He'd been chosen for a special job, he'd been told, and was as pleased as punch when he learned what it was all about. He liked Mrs Footlong, but he wasn't so keen on his driver who was given to giggling because she realised he'd been allocated the booby prize rather than the trophy, and was amazed at how seriously he was taking it.

"Thomas, next week, Chief Inspector I shouldn't wonder. You'll be fast-tracked after this, like." And she cackled in a most unpleasant manner.

"Don't be silly, Em. Anyway, what are you going to do while I'm interviewing Mrs Footlong?"

"I shall be having a good look round, perhaps talk to some of the natives, maybe look for clues." He sensed the sarcasm, but ignored it. His feeling of pride extended to being driven to the appointment, rather like having a chauffeur he thought, just like the Chief Constable. Wait till he told his mum and dad!

"You got a girlfriend, Thomas?"

"No. No I haven't. Bit shy, Em. Not good with girls." This was music to Emily's ears. She'd always dreamed of getting her hands on a shy bloke and awakening every sense he possessed. Why not try her luck with Thomas? He must be ripe for plucking.

"How do you fancy a date, like, I mean, go out together, you and me?" He nearly slid off his seat, went bright red and turned to face the side window. "Go on mate, how about it?"

"Em …. urm … Em … that's, that's so nice, and yes I'd like that very much, thank you."

"Great. We'll arrange it after your mission here. And here we are. Little Scampering. Now do you know where Mrs F lives?" He did and directed her straight to it. "Cool. I'll park outside and have a wander. Good luck, Thomas." He thanked her, disembarked, and headed for the door.

***

Sally Cainton's chest was also swelling with pride. Her feature had been so successful to the paper she'd been given a rise, a handsome bonus, and her stature as a journalist had increased several-fold.

There had been an anonymous phone call. A villager, who claimed to be able to lift the lid further on Little Scampering, unmasking wrong-doers of many persuasions, as well as revealing perpetrators of naughty goings-on had told her to meet them in a field near the village after dark. This was easily dismissed. Sally wasn't going to meet *anybody* alone in a field at night! It was pointless mentioning the call to the police, this probably being the work of a crank, and the police, on past experience, wouldn't be interested anyway.

The 'crank' in this case was the killer, a person who could not afford to be thwarted. Back to the drawing board!

***

As he expected PC Bowlman was shown into the lounge and bade to sit, and offered a drink, hot or cold. He elected for neither. Edith observed he was sitting quite upright as if he was nervous, which he probably was, but mostly because he wanted to appear totally professional, of that she was sure.

"Thank you, Mrs Footlong," quoth he, "I'll just get my notebook out and then we can begin, if you are ready, of course."

"Yes I am, thank you, Thomas." She waited, relaxed further into her own chair, and crossed her legs. He looked up and smiled, such an angelic smile, she thought, and she acknowledged that was her signal.

"First I must ask you some questions, but I know you will not be able to answer me, so may we please take that as read?" His

128

smile effectively said yes. "One, was Mrs Merde's body left in a, shall we say, neat and tidy position?" He looked shocked for a second or two and then replied.

"As agreed, Mrs Footlong, I cannot answer." He hadn't blinked. But suddenly his eyes shot to the floor and back up again in an instant. Edith's heart missed a beat. Was he sending a message? She tried her next question.

"Has that fact been made public, Thomas? Is it general knowledge?" She waited patiently and when nothing occurred she began to wonder if she'd misread the situation. His eyes remained steadily on hers. But then they swept from side to side in a brief movement before locking back onto Edith's. Yes, she'd read it aright! That was a no, and that is what she hoped.

"I've spoken to Mr Merde more than once and he has maintained that he couldn't go out onto the patio, he was too shocked, and something was holding him back. He couldn't even go out when the 999 operator asked him to. It was dark, they had no outside lights, and he couldn't see clearly, the position only slightly improving when he switched the lounge lights on. It is conceivable that he didn't realise her body had been neatly arranged. We cannot begin to imagine his horror faced by such a gruesome discovery, or how shattered he felt seeing his beloved wife lying there murdered, assuming him to be innocent, and I think he is.

"Do the police agree with my assessment, do you know?" She stared hard at him waiting for the signal. When it came it was a barely discernible shrug of the shoulders. Perhaps she'd asked too much in one go.

"If he is innocent, do you believe he couldn't go out on the patio?" Again a shrug. Ah, thought Edith, these are details he has no knowledge of. "Very well, I will give you my findings, Thomas, and I do understand why you haven't answered a single question." He smiled sweetly again.

***

Thomas had come merely to take Edith's statement, but held her in the highest regard, mainly because she reminded him so much of his dear, beloved granny, so that he wanted to help in

129

any way he could. Apart from anything else he wanted the police to solve the crime and was emboldened in his task because he'd been entrusted to do his job and do it particularly well. He was determined to act the detective as that was what he wanted to be, and if Edith had vital evidence he, Thomas Bowlman, could play an active part in what happened next.

Of course, he held the DCI is equal regard and had, for a while, been reluctant to pass on any information he shouldn't. But he did know about the body and also that its arrangement had not been disclosed to the media or the public generally. So how could he help Edith? What he couldn't say might be essential to her own investigation. There had to be a way, hence the eventual use of his eyes, an operation that could be easily denied if need be. Now he relaxed, sat back, crossed his own legs and raised his pen ready to write.

***

"When I interviewed other residents," Edith got under way, "I spoke about my interest in improving the community spirit, which was mostly well received, and then casually mentioned the murder in passing. I obtained a variety of responses as you might well imagine! Although some were genuine concerned about Mr Merde stumbling on his dead wife in that manner, and how it may have affected him, nobody went any further, except one.

"It was Mrs Trumpling at the pub, Thomas. She said it was sick to arrange the corpse in such a manner, well, neat and tidy I think she said. Bad enough killing someone without fiddling with their body afterwards, that was the gist of her words. She was the only person to bring that up. It was clear nobody else knew anything beyond the basic news that Mrs Merde had been stabbed on her patio.

"Now I accept Mrs Trumpling *might* have heard that elsewhere, but I cannot imagine that to be true. If Carl saw so little and was so distressed I do not believe he could've described it, so it can't have come from him. All this hinges, of course, on how much the police have said.

"Finally, the motive. I think this was a crime of passion if I have the correct term. Almost certainly Mr Trumpling was seeing

Mrs Merde on the quiet and Mrs Trumpling found out. I was talking to Mr Trumpling and it was he who raised the matter of infidelity, joking about his wife dealing with him and his lover if he was ever caught going astray. Only I don't think he was joking, Thomas. Just something in his attitude, if you understand me, his expression, and there was a coldness about him. I can't explain it better than that."

Thomas nodded and closed his notebook. Then he opened it again and read through all he had written. Edith watched him in silence.

"Thank you, Mrs Footlong. I'll report back to DCI Mehedren and let you know. But I must ask you not to speak of this to anyone for the time being. That is vital."

"I appreciate that, Thomas, and my lips are sealed. I shall await your report."

***

Thomas rejoined Emily Coombes who was waiting in the car outside.

"You're not going to believe this," he began.

Chapter Twenty Three

Deepak and Poojah Nagarka had called in on Roger Kempson who was making an excellent recovery and enjoying the company of any passing villagers who bothered to knock. And there were many.

Roger had asked Nancy Harmand to get him a small gift for his saviour, small because she wouldn't have appreciated anything larger or more extravagant. At a loss Nancy had approached Grace who suggested afternoon tea for two at the Chilston Park hotel, and Nancy swiftly arranged the voucher, thinking it sounded a splendid idea, especially as Grace had sampled said refreshments.

Poojah, being modest, was overcome by the 'thank you' card alone that Roger now presented her with, and that was nothing compared to her reaction when the gift voucher dropped out. Reduced to tears she hugged Roger and told him he was a very naughty boy!

Another lady in receipt of an act of kindness was Belinda Thredsham to whom was delivered a bouquet of flowers with a note 'from a group of well-wishers in the village in the hope you are Mr Parkforth remain here as one of us'. Although anonymous it was a heart-warming gesture.

Gradually the bad that was done by the reporter was undone, even Francesca Towford benefiting from this new understanding following her meeting with Edith.

Yet still the murder hung over them. From the police, silence. Carl remained uncharged and at large, and the longer that went on the less guilty he appeared. There was increased support for the theory that the killer was an outsider, but perhaps this was the result of residents trying to sub-consciously wrap themselves in a safety net by not admitting it could be one of their number.

Apart from Grace they mostly remained in ignorance of Edith's investigative work. But not all were so. Among those alerted to her efforts was the killer.

***

Thomas Bowlman typed up his report, added his own comments, and was now standing before DS Willie Broughton.

"Thank you for this, Thomas. Excellent. You did well." Thomas blushed, not appreciating the DS was being sarcastic. But then Willie had wanted to appear genuine and was pleased that he had succeeded. "I'll show this to the DCI, we'll take whatever action we deem necessary, and I'll let you know if due course. Please advise Mrs Footlong of that, and say we will ring her in the next few days." Thomas thanked him and went off to make the call.

Willie smiled, then giggled, then laughed out loud. As he was alone he carried out an imaginary arrest of Mrs Trumpling.

"Mrs Trumpling, your husband had an extra-marital relationship with the deceased, Mrs Alana Merde, and you took your revenge by murdering Mrs Merde. Is that correct? Come now, Mrs Trumpling, of course you did. Mrs Footlong says so. Own up or I shall have to torture you...."

"Practising Willie? How will you torture her?" Lucy Panshaw, hearing a voice, had crept into the room unnoticed. "Waterboarding? Flogging with a cat-o-nine-tails? Or will you let her go if she offers you free beer for the next year?" Willie was as red as Thomas had been earlier.

"Okay, okay, take the .... whatever. Have a glance at this then you'll know why I'm being silly." Lucy read it through a couple of times and looked at Willie with a serious expression.

"Willie, you're right. We may have to torture her ..."

"Yep, well, anyway, I have to decide whether or not to present this to auntie Sheelagh. She told me to file it away somewhere dark and inaccessible. Your shout, Lucy, do I stay or do I go?"

"Go Willie go. Just for a laugh. She'll see the funny side."

"And if she doesn't?"

"Well, you'll be mincemeat, won't you?" and she slipped through the door, saying over her shoulder, "as usual!" He threw a pencil at the closing door and heard her laugh as she disappeared down the corridor. Then he chuckled.

***

Alison Digbin wished she had something to laugh about. She wished she'd never married Peter, but then she often wished that. She thought she'd found a real man, a super-hero. He was all macho, very confident, handsome, well-groomed, smart dresser; he was a catch, for it seemed all the girls were after him.

And he chose her! All her dreams come true. He'd told her she'd never need to work, he'd always provide for her and then, of course, there'd be children. Children! But she found out too late she couldn't have children. By then he'd changed anyway.

The beatings had started.

She was little more than a slave. She couldn't tell anyone, not her mother or sister, because there was always the chance they'd tell him, and then she'd suffer. In recent times she'd read in the papers and magazines about men like him, and about how there was help and support available these days. But she didn't dare, and she tried to shield herself from the worst by thinking that he did indeed provide for her, that she had all the clothes she wanted, a nice home, and they took good holidays.

But it was an oppressive life. Few friends of her own, for he frowned on such relationships, although it was alright for him to have his many friends, and for her to play the dutiful wife when those mates came round. Listen to their crude jokes, listen to the endless debates and arguments about football and cricket, listen to their infantile masculine banter. And smile. And laugh. And provide refreshments.

He gave her enough money, but that was double-edged, for she had responsibility for making sure there was always plenty of alcohol in stock. He'd punched her once for getting the wrong lager in.

However, her new friendship with Edith was not condemned as she thought it might be. For one thing it would ensure the garden was up to scratch, another aspect of his control over her, and she was looking forward to some happy times ahead. Happy times in a sad life.

Carl! God forbid he should ever find out about Carl. Carl had been so understanding and sympathetic, and had wanted to give Peter a good hiding. Carl said she didn't have to put up with it, just as the papers and magazines said, but what good was that?

She was the one in trouble, not they. And still she could see no way out, no end to her misery.

***

Lucy and Hassana were taking a short stroll not far from HQ to allow Hassana the opportunity to talk over certain concerns.

"It's like this, Lucy, I can't help my feelings, my emotions, but I think I can cope with what I might see doing this job, what I might come across, but I don't think it'll stop me getting emotions as it were. Sorry, not explaining well."

"Yes you are. They're your words, that's all that matters."

"Well, you remember that lass in Dover and her baby son, Noah, and the fact she was making ends meet by being on the game, well, that really upset me, and I wanted to cry for her. I did shed a few tears when I was alone. Then that poor old lady that was nearly killed, and was saved by that guy who just happened along at the right moment, well, things like that affect me."

Lucy recalled the investigation into Gareth Modlum's murder and how his killer targeted the woman who could identify him, saved in the nick of time by Clayton Mainstreet, if she remembered the name right. It wasn't their finest hour. The police were slow, in her opinion, but then she knew command wasn't that easy, and that sometimes decisions are made depending on the known situation at the time. Hassana was still speaking:

"I know we're supposed to be sort of, like, cold and aloof, and not show our feelings, least of all to the public, but that's the bit of police work that I'm finding difficult to live with. I really don't think I'd let my emotions get the better of me in an incident, I hope I'd act as a professional, like, but it plays on my mind, and I just needed to talk to someone. Sorry it's you, Lucy."

"Don't be sorry. No apologies. Pleased you felt you could chat about it with me. And it's fine to do that, Hassana. Talk. Best way sometimes. Best way of letting your true feelings out. What you're expressing is the thoughts of many officers, especially early in their careers. I could identify with what you were saying, as I went through that myself. Only a few officers, as far as I know, get immune to it, and only then after years of service.

135

"And you'll find the DCI more approachable than you might think! But is anything on the Little Scampering murder troubling you right now?"

"Just how she was murdered, y'know, stabbed straight through the heart, her body arranged, and left for her husband to find her. I don't know about you but I don't kinda think he did it. But what bothers me is that another villager might have, and that I might have spoken to that person. Did I do enough, ask the right questions, that sort of thing?"

"Believe me, Hassana, you did. You did what was asked of you, simple as that, and being the good detective you are you would've been alerted to anything that needed picking up on." They shared a pleasant smile. "Well, better get back to the coal face."

"Yeah, thanks for your time. Mean it."

"Know you do, and you're welcome."

***

The approachable DCI was not a description Willie Broughton would've applied to his boss when taking PC Bowlman's report to her.

"And why do you think I need to see this, precisely?"

"Thought you might like a laugh, ma'am."

"I told you to file it. Would you like *me* to file it? I can think of somewhere it will fit very snuggly. And then I can have a good laugh."

"Sorry ma'am."

"Let it ride a couple of days and then phone her and say we've looked into it and there's insufficient evidence to proceed further. Gawd, we don't need to tangle this up any more. Right, for your penance you can say ten Hail Sheelaghs and buy me a pint next time we're in a pub. And no, not in the *Downsman*!"

***

"Grace," enquired Edith, looking suitably puzzled, "any idea what a native of Little Scampering is called? A Scamp? A Scamperer? Any ideas?"

136

"Goodness me, no I haven't. I'm happy being a maid of Kent, that'll do me. Maybe you should do a poll of villagers. I expect someone who thinks they have expert knowledge will come up with something astounding! By the way, did you see the police?"

"Oh yes, PC Bowlman came. I didn't expect DCI Mehedren to come in person, but I'd have thought they'd be here investigating by now."

"Go on, Edith, who did it?" And Edith explained her theory without naming the culprit, much to Grace's annoyance, leaving Grace open mouthed. "Well I never, Edith, who'd have thought that? So who was it, do tell?"

"The police do not want me to mention that to anyone. I'm sure you'll understand. PC Bowlman, Thomas, such a nice young man, restores your faith in the youth of today, well, he said they'd call in a day or two so I suppose I must wait to hear."

But before she heard Edith was destined to be overtaken by events.

In the meantime August had rolled on, hot as ever, and the second heatwave had taken its toll just before the middle of the month. Now, quite suddenly rain appeared on the forecast, which didn't feel confident to commit itself to where it would fall in Kent, or by how much.

"Ridiculous," Edith commented, sharply, "all those experts, all that expensive equipment, and they can't say accurately where and when rain may fall, but they can tell you exactly what the climate will be like in thirty years time!"

"I know, I know," Grace responded, trying to sound sympathetic, "but we must take climate change seriously, Edith."

"Yes, and I do, you may rely upon it." Edith smiled at her friend who returned the gesture and then offered her guest some nearly frozen water, readily accepted.

137

Chapter Twenty Four

They'd prayed for rain. They'd prayed for weeks, no, months and at last they received a small gift, a downpour. It didn't last long, but it was heavenly, and it was a downpour by any definition. Those who loved the sun wished it was only a temporary diversion, whereas those who loved their garden or whose health was suffering wished it would last forever.

It came one evening. Not all of Kent was affected and of those who were blessed with such water the quantity varied appreciably. Little Scampering, atop the Downs, got a decent soaking. Grace had returned home from Edith's, where she'd spent the evening, just before the clouds deposited some of their moisture earthwards.

"Ah," she sighed, peacefully, "God's got his watering can out."

Edith had to close her patio doors but was able to leave the windows at the front open, for it was still too warm to close up, and there she sat and enjoyed the sight and sounds as day became twilight and twilight became night.

Unfortunately, it didn't last into the night, the sound of rain falling ceasing, to be replaced by various drips as trees, shrubs, plants and leaky gutters let the sweet nectar drop to the ground. The next sound Edith heard was a distant cry of 'come here, bad dog, come here, heel, come here' and she smiled at the thought of a neighbour trying to round up an escaped hound.

But then there was an uncanny sound which she barely heard at first. It was almost ghostly, and she now tried to listen intently. And then it became a clear voice, seemingly, so she reasoned, a woman's voice.

"Eeeeeeeeeeeeedith ...... Eeeeeeeeeeeedith .... Eeeeeeeeeeeeedith"

A sudden thought struck her. Was it someone in trouble? Had someone slipped over and hurt themselves?

"Eeeeeeeeeeeeedith ..." It sounded more pained and urgent. She had to go and investigate, and she put the porch light on and set off. No more than two or three steps along the path she shuddered and was conscious of some sort of presence. Edith instinctively spun round and there it was, a dark, shadowy figure, black cloak, black hood, or so it appeared in the dark, and in its hand something that glinted, something long and thin. In that split second she knew it was a knife but was rendered motionless with fear, unable to move, unable to scream, and knew her last moment had come. Was it Felicity Trumpling come to silence her?

***

Nancy Harmand was enjoying some respite, able to breathe easily or more easily than of late, but it was still too hot, the rain doing nothing to ease that. But it was something. And she was bathing in happy memories of another wonderful evening spent with Ken. Tonight they had shared a warm, tender kiss, enthralling in its gentleness, a moment of splendid pleasure, a magical moment that was a treasure in itself. She recalled the thrill that surged through her body as their lips met and his arms engulfed her.

This was paradise. This isn't just for the young, she decided. Passion had overrun them and they had feverishly hugged and squeezed and caressed as their lips melted into one beautiful absorbing kiss. What a climax to such an evening!

She'd wanted him to stay the night but couldn't bring herself to ask. He would've accepted had she known it, and so they parted later, happy but sad all at the same time.

He'd floated down to the gate, waved to Nancy on the doorstep and set a course for home, almost bumping into Philip Plusmith going the other way with his dog, Fido, in tow. As they greeted each other Fido took the opportunity to slip his lead, as he was apt to do, and Philip had to excuse himself and set off after the miscreant canine.

"Come back, come back, Fido. Bad dog. Come back, come back, heel, damn you!" he yelled as Fido made good his escape. Every time Philip got close Fido would set off.

"You've got him well trained," Mr Sonnel called out sarcastically as they passed. Then Fido turned up someone's front garden and an exasperated owner bellowed after him, ordering him back, telling him he was such a bad boy.

Fido added to his transgression by barking ferociously, an action sure to annoy the neighbour, or so Mr Plusmith thought. In fact, Fido had just saved a life.

Edith could see nothing but death when a piercing bark thrust its way into her ears. The black figure had stepped forward ready to stab its victim when Fido chanced upon the scene, leaping at the devil in front of her. It was enough. The figure vanished while the dog stood guard in front of Edith barking for all it was worth.

Mr Plusmith arrived ready to take poor Fido to task, but Edith was already gathering her senses. She collapsed on the ground and Philip rushed to her aid.

"Did he attack you?" he shouted.

"No, Mr Plusmith, he saved my life," she whimpered. It would be difficult to understand who was the most shocked. Philip Plusmith looked around uncomprehending. "Mr Plusmith I was about to be attacked with a knife and Fido came to my rescue. He's my saviour, my hero," she gasped before fainting.

***

When she came round she found she was safe and Philip had everything under control. He'd had his mobile with him and had hit 999 instantly before carrying Edith indoors where she was licked lovingly by Fido until he was ordered to stop. A little later and she had more company with a paramedic checking her over, and DC Sian Stramer taking the details of the incident.

Edith explained about the way her name had been called from outside, about the hooded figure and the knife, and about how Fido saved her. Sian was not aware of Edith's piece of criminal investigation and listened incredulously, wondering why the team had not been notified, but as the tale unfurled she realised that Edith's work had not been taken seriously. And she realised why.

So, was this dark figure actually a figment of Edith's imagination? Could be. Yet there was the dog's reaction. But maybe Fido was simply, playfully, greeting Mrs Footlong. Time to call in.

DS Willie Broughton listened carefully and said he'd come out, if the DCI approved. Sheelagh was not in the mood to approve and give some degree of credence to Edith's witterings, as she called them. But Lucy spoke up.

"Ma'am, if it's the killer, just suppose it's the killer, we need to be there, we need to try, we need to be seen to be protecting the public."

"And wasting our time, Lucy. She's decided who the murderer is and has now seen a blinking ghost, or thinks she has. For God's sake, let's get real."

"No. You're wrong, ma'am. Let's look into it and if we find a big zero, that's it. Over and done with, full stop." Sheelagh stared at her in the silence that had enveloped the incident room. You could feel the tension, it was utterly tangible. Hassana winced. You've gone too far, Lucy, she thought, dreading what was to follow. Finally the DCI spoke.

"Full marks for standing up to me, Lucy. You'll go far. It takes a woman to have that strength of purpose and I applaud you, and I would tell you in no uncertain terms if I thought you were wrong. I don't agree with you but we'll run with it. Well argued, Lucy, well argued. Okay gang, let's get organised.

***

And so the police descended on Little Scampering en masse.

But this time they found a clue, a small, precious clue, something denied them when Mrs Merde met her end, the ground having then been baked solid.

They found a footprint on the flowerbed to one side of where Edith had been attacked. A large footprint in soil recently moistened by the downpour. Probably a man's footprint, but make no assumptions. Sheelagh immediately ordered a door-to-door throughout the village with the instructions that she wanted to know exactly, exactly mind, what every person was doing in the hour leading up to Edith's brush with death.

Within the hour enquiries were complete. Felicity Trumpling had been in the pub all evening, a fact verified by the other staff as well as a number of local customers. Up to a point this eliminated her from the list of potential suspects, and therefore eliminated her from Edith's findings.

Had Edith imagined it all? There was Fido, of course, and there was the footprint. But everyone seemed to have an alibi, even if not all were watertight, or verifiable.

Hassana Achebe had interviewed some of the residents, a few having been woken from their slumbers, and something was worrying her, but she couldn't put her finger on it. Lucy's words about being a good detective came back to her, and she knew she'd seen something relevant but couldn't decide what. And then it hit her.

"Ma'am," she called out, like someone who has just seen the light, "if you please. The Digbins. I called there and both said they'd been in watching telly all evening. Not been out. They asked what it was all about and he became indignant when I said we couldn't say at this stage. Said they'd hardly stirred from their lounge, except to go to the toilet. Well, there was a small piece of mud on the hall floor and Mr Digbin had a piece of mud on the side of his shoe."

"Well, it had only rained for a short while tonight. The ground was rock hard. Where did that mud come from if they stayed indoors?"

Sheelagh slipped off the desk she'd been propped up on, eyes wide awake.

"Brilliant Hassana. Right, let's do him. I want every shoe he possesses nabbed and checked, and checked against that footprint. Okay, let's sort out orders."

Chapter Twenty Five

Once again the benighted residents of this rural hamlet were awakened by police cars and the police officers swarming everywhere, not that many could see very much, it being a moonless night and there being no street lights.

Gradually those officers called at every house. Although it was late most people were awake if not actually dressed. There was a degree of annoyance and indignation from certain quarters but generally folk guessed it might have something to do with the murder and took to it all with an element of excitement. Phones glowed red hot as calls to neighbours were made.

But in time it all slowed up. However, that was about the time it accelerated for the Digbins.

The DCI, in no mood for any nonsense, but all too aware they could be making a mistake, stormed up the Digbin's drive with Willie Broughton and Hassana Achebe in hot pursuit. Their prey had retired but, like the other villagers, were waiting for developments little realising they would be centre stage. Peter was not happy when the doorbell rang and issued forth with an array of unpleasant language largely comprised of obscene adjectives, verbs and foul anatomical nouns. Alison was already shaking as she climbed out of bed and put a dressing gown on. Peter had slipped into a track suit. He threw open the front door where Sheelagh thrust her ID into his face.

"Look, we've been questioned, now you're waking us again. I've got to drive a train first thing today, for heaven's sake."

"May we come in?" Sheelagh bellowed at him as she entered the property anyway and came face to face with her adversary. Confronted with the considerable presence of the DCI, Peter backed away, which Sheelagh took to mean 'come in'. Alison had arrived, looking pale and frightened, and asked what was happening. The DCI replied before Peter could speak.

"Let's come in the lounge, please. Don't want to do this here on the doorstep, now do we? It's alright, Mrs Digbin, we have some questions and an unusual request."

Alison guided them into the lounge while Peter stood to one side, silent, but obviously seething inside. Slowly they all took their seats except for Willie, who appeared to be guarding the door.

"Right. When DC Achebe called earlier you insisted you'd been indoors all evening watching telly, only going out for the toilet. Is that right?" Alison looked so afraid she appeared as if she might burst into tears.

"Look, what's this all about?" Peter asked, aggressively.

"Answer the question, please."

"Yes, alright then. Yes, that's right."

"Neither of you went outside?"

"No, of course not. It'd been pouring with bleedin' rain, hadn't it? No need to go outside. We're civilised, we've got an indoor toilet." His anger was turning to raw sarcasm.

"DC Achebe reported mud in your hall and on one of your shoes, Mr Digbin. Would you mind showing us the shoes you were wearing at that point?"

"What?" he yelled. He looked ready to explode, Alison ready to swoon.

"I think you heard me. I am obtaining a search warrant," she fibbed, "so why not co-operate, Mr Digbin? If you have done no wrong you have nothing to fear, do you? If you don't mind me saying so, you're acting suspiciously, aren't you?" Alison couldn't cope with this any longer.

"Peter, Peter, whatever have you done?" she squealed, throwing her hands to her face.

"Shut it, shut it, you stupid cow," he screamed. But she would not be silenced, not this time. She'd taken enough.

"You went out for a walk, you told me, and then you told the officer we'd stayed in all evening, and I……"

"Shut it, now," he roared, leaping from his seat with every appearance of someone about to launch an assault. Willie stepped in smartly and Peter made the mistake of swinging a punch at the Sergeant. Willie wrestled him to the ground while Alison did indeed faint.

***

144

Peace was soon restored and the DCI radioed for back-up while Hassana applied her first aid skills to reviving Alison. Peter was handcuffed, arrested and carted off, Willie in attendance. Sheelagh remained, anxious to speak to Alison as soon as the woman felt able.

"Alison, when you're ready, and there's no rush, please tell me your story." Another officer had gone to make tea, a mug of which Alison cuddled while she improved to the point that she was ready.

"My husband is a brute, a wife-beater. After this officer called tonight," she nodded towards Hassana, sitting next to her, "he made it clear I was never to say he'd been out. He punched me in the stomach, slapped my face, held me down and walloped me. I didn't dare ask him what it was all about, he'd have only hit me more." Hassana was nearly in tears and just managed to hold them back.

"What is it about? Please tell me what he's done wrong."

"I think you should prepare yourself for a shock. But first, do you know if your husband knew Alana Merde more closely than as a neighbour?" Sheelagh was speaking softly and quietly, but her words still alarmed Alison.

"Oh God, what's he done, what's he done?"

"Did he know her, Mrs Digbin? And may I call you Alison?" She nodded.

"He never said anything to me. I don't think he did. But even if I'd wondered I wouldn't have dreamed of asking. He was a violent man."

"When we first interviewed the village in the immediate aftermath of the killing, Mr Digbin said he'd left late that evening to go on duty. We've checked. That was a lie, Alison." The poor woman's shoulders started to heave and the tears came, and she was shaking and trembling.

"I didn't know, I swear I didn't know…."

"I believe you, Alison. Would you like to rest now?" She shook her head, and made an effort to control herself.

"You must understand I could never ask him any questions about what he did. He never hesitated to hit me. Look." And she rose and lifted her dressing gown so they could see the ugly red weals on her buttocks, sitting down again while Hassana gasped

145

and let a teardrop escape and run down her left cheek. But Alison was gaining strength.

"I am very sorry, Alison," Sheelagh said, with real feeling and compassion. She felt just as Hassana did. "Tonight we have reason to believe he went out to attack Mrs Edith Footlong, possibly with the intention of killing her, as he may have thought she knew something he wanted kept hidden. Do you mind if we search your house now?"

Alison was pulling herself together, having guessed it was something horrible.

"Yes, please go ahead. And he did come home with mud on his shoes. I saw it in the hall after this officer came, but I wouldn't have said anything to him. I just quietly cleared it up." Her head sunk and there was another flow of tears. Sheelagh and Hassana felt for her, ached for her, wanted to ease her pain and suffering, wanted to make it all better. Hassana was left to cuddle the forlorn Alison and all her own tears fell in that moment. The DCI organised the search, close to tears herself.

They ascertained there was no close family but discovered Alison had recently formed a friendship with Edith. Sian Stramer paid a call on Mrs Footlong who was very surprised to find a police officer back on her doorstep in the middle of the night. She readily agreed to take in Alison Digbin who was transferred from her own home while the search took place. Sian was confident that might be the case, and Edith treated her like her own daughter while the distressed woman treated Edith like her mum. Sian was delighted and, as agreed, remained with the two ladies for the time being.

146

Chapter Twenty Six

With Peter Digbin in custody, and already charged with attempted assault on a police officer, he knew the game was up. He asked for a solicitor and said he would make a full confession, at the same time absolving his wife of any involvement, which was just about the only kind gesture he'd shown Alison for many a year. Nonetheless, she had to be brought in for questioning but was soon released, and was picked up by her parents and taken to their home.

The story Peter had to tell was told in unpleasant fashion, as befitting such a man, but was quite revealing and remarkable for all that.

Edith and Sian had tucked Alison up in bed where she was asleep in no time, but her rest was disturbed by nightmares that produced screams, tears, and cold sweats. But she was attended by good comforters, who themselves were finally able to catch some shut-eye before the dawn.

Little Scampering was buzzing but as yet few knew the truth.

Sally Cainton was alerted and, being thick-skinned, decided she needn't worry about the villagers, she'd plough straight in. In the event she had to plough straight out again. Nobody would talk to her. Nobody at all. And then it happened.

Another anonymous phone call, this time suggesting they meet on a footpath near the village, close to some woods, when a whole raft of stories would be passed over. With the killer arrested Sally naturally assumed that she was safe and was so keen to progress her expose, especially as there might be more gossip allied to Peter Digbin involved, that she thought it was an opportunity too good to miss. A handful of extra juicy tidbits, gleaned from whatever the caller had to say, might be the perfect tonic!

But by making the arrangement had Sally actually entered into a potentially lethal pact?

***

Once the duty solicitor had been located and brought in, and after a private talk with Peter, they were ready to roll, Willie and Lucy one side of the table facing their quarry and Amelia Threekings. Willie knew Ms Threekings of old. It was a good job Mr Digbin was confessing and they might not be required to question him in any great detail, for Amelia took her work seriously and would be ready to leap to his rescue in a trice.

But Peter Digbin managed to make her wince more than once, mainly with his terminology, which, at first, brought hidden smiles to the Detective Sergeants.

"Well, it's like this," he began as he settled back in his seat, "I wanted to see old Merde about a bit of carpentry, nothing elaborate, I'd heard he wasn't good at anything complicated. So I told Alison I'd pop in on my afternoon walk. It was my day off. In fact I went there first. Carl Merde was up in London with his son and she, Alana that is, greeted me, and she was wearing next to nothing.

"I thought, well now, she's a bit cheeky, but I introduced myself, explained what I wanted and she invited me in. Well, I thought, be rude not to, but once inside she started getting all seductive, if you follow me, and she nestled up to me and I could feel the warmth of her body, and her perfume was intoxicating, I can tell you."

"Mr Digbin," interrupted Amelia, looking perplexed, "this is a formal statement, it doesn't have to be so graphic." Willie dared not look at Lucy who was, in any case, studying the ceiling.

"Oh, okay, right. Well, we started kissing, you know how these things happen, and before we knew what was happening we were in the bedroom. She flung herself on the bed, arms and legs wide apart, just like I arranged her when I knifed her, and said to me 'how would you like to drive your train into my tunnel – the signals are green – come on, let's couple-up' and I was so taken that I dived ...."

"Mr Digbin!" Amelia exclaimed, loudly and clearly.

"Oh ... oh ... sorry ... right ... well, we made love. At the height of her passion she cried out 'all aboard – mind the gap – woooo woooo!' and that just inspired me more ...."

"I wish to speak alone with my client," declared Ms Threekings, vexation covering her countenance.

Willie granted the request and exited with Lucy in tow, going a safe distance down the corridor before dissolving into fits of giggles.

***

Cometh the hour, cometh the phone call. It was early evening and Sally we preparing for departure when her anonymous contact rang to change the time and venue. She was advised to be in the Digbins' front garden just after nightfall.

"You can park outside, of course. Hope you find that reassuring." Sally had not been able to assess whether the caller was male or female, but the voice was probably disguised anyway, and now she had more hope than before. In truth, she was excited, the adrenalin was flowing. This anonymous person could well be Alison Digbin, ready to spill more beans than you could hope to count. It was almost a case of 'hold the front page'. She'd get her own back on these reticent villagers who had blanked her after Peter Digbin was arrested.

So she was quite pleased it was dark when she drove into the village and allowed her electric car to glide all but silently up to its destination. By now she was positively on-fire with enthusiasm, and she made her eager way up the garden path where the house remained in complete darkness. No notice was taken of the bushes that lined the path. She was on her way to a scoop.

She reached the front doorstep and turned to see a terrifying sight immediately behind her. Sally could barely make out the figure in the dark but there was no mistaking the blade of the knife just inches from her.

***

When Willie and Lucy returned to the interview room they came upon a very different Peter Digbin. He was almost cowering in the corner, rather subdued, and Amelia Threekings was looking bright and smarmy. Clearly she'd explained the situation to the accused, possibly in words of one syllable, most definitely in manner he would understand, and had managed to temper his descriptions to the point where his discourse became quite boring. But not for long.

"Mrs Merde," he said, softly and deliberately, "thanked me for being good company and asked if she could take a selfie, just a souvenir of a happy occasion, not a photo to be shared with her husband, of course. I was so happy I agreed. Worst days work I could've done. Anyways, she takes the picture of us lying together ... um .... undressed on the bed. And that was that. I went home, having left my phone number for Car ... um ... Mr Merde to ring.

"Not long after I had a call from her saying that she wanted a thousand pounds cash to delete the picture or my wife would get to see it. I was in a state. I didn't know if she really meant it, but I got so worked up, took it out on Ali, and decided I'd got to deal with Ala ... um ... Mrs Merde."

Lucy listened with such sadness you could almost sense tears forming. Her face was a picture of sorrow, yet inside there was a burning rage. He took it out on Ali, he'd said. An innocent woman beaten by a controlling bully over something that wasn't her fault.

"Well, cut a long story short, I arranged to meet her that night and hand over the dosh. I told Ali I was working, drove out of the village and parked where I wouldn't be seen and waited. Dozed a bit, otherwise just sat and waited. Then during the night I wandered up to her place, through the side gate she'd left open and waited on the patio.

"Then she appeared, dressed to kill. Er, sorry. Not a good choice of words. She came up to me but stopped a few feet away. I don't know what that is in metres. Feet and inches man, me. She said, fancy a repeat, out here on the warm patio? All aboard the midnight express! I said that I'd got the money and I wasn't there to give her a guaranteed connection ...."

"Mr Digbin!" cried an exasperated Amelia.

"Oh yes, sorry, sorry. Anyways I dropped the envelope with the money, except it wasn't the dosh at all, right at her feet. She bent down to pick it up and as she stood up I thrust the old knife I'd got right up into her heart." Willie saw Amelia wince and involuntarily pull a face. "The day before I'd been to the doctor, different matter, and got her to show me exactly where the heart is. Useful that. How to murder someone on the NHS ..."

"Mr Digbin!"

"Yeah, well, sorry. After I'd done her I arranged her all nice, just like the way she'd sprawled on the bed that day. That'll teach you, you evil little ..."

"MR DIGBIN!"

"Thought I'd got away with it, then I learned that Edith Footlong woman had worked out who the killer was and I realised I'd got to do her as well. Bloody dog stopped me. Why do people have dogs, I ask you?" Willie leaned forward and placed his arms on the table.

"Well now, Peter, Edith Footlong did *not* identify you. She thought it was someone quite different. So if you hadn't attacked her you might indeed have got away with it. How does it feel, as an insignificant, unintelligent form of pondlife, now that you've been exposed as a complete plonker? And if I had my way wife-beaters would be hanged, drawn and quartered."

"Sergeant!" Amelia interrupted.

"I'd be very sorry to hear that you feel differently, Ms Threekings." Lucy, now almost smiling, was inwardly applauding. Well done, Willie. After a pause Amelia spoke.

"I have decided to ignore your remarks and will not be making a complaint." Willie took this to mean that she didn't feel differently.

The interview was now nearly over. Lucy's stomach had turned and she learned later that Willie's had too.

"You handled the pair of 'em brilliantly, DS Broughton," she commended when they were alone, "and your comments, wow, hit him right between the eyes, I saw how much it hurt him."

"I'd have hurt him alright if I could've got hold of him." And they shared sad grins as Lucy took his arm and hugged it tight.

"My hero," she said.

***

Sally screamed and automatically stepped backwards, tripping up the doorstep and landing against the front door with a thump. But in that instant the blade had vanished and there was the muffled sounds of a struggle. Suddenly she realised, even in the dark, her assailant was being tackled by a rescuer.

"Can you help me, miss?" a voice cried, "and sit on his legs while I handcuff him." Heavens be praised! It had to be a policeman, and it was. PC Thomas Bowlman, left to patrol the village in the aftermath of events, had seen Sally go into the garden and, knowing nobody was home, came over to acquaint her with the fact, whereupon he caught sight of the attacker and wrestled him to the ground.

Now Sally was holding onto the legs very firmly while Thomas applied the handcuffs behind the man's back. Once secure Thomas brought his torch out as he spoke.

"Right, let's turn him over and see who we have this time. Is that alright with you, miss? Sorry, I haven't asked if you're okay. Are you?"

"I am, I am. And yes, let's turn him over." And turn him over they did. Thomas shone the torch in his face and that's when they had a shock. Their prisoner was as adept with issuing profanities as Carl allegedly was, and swore horribly obscene oaths largely relating to body parts and what could be done with them.

Their prisoner was not a man after all, it was Belinda Thredsham. Thomas radioed in and yet once more Little Scampering was invaded by the police. As Grace later remarked:

"Don't know why the police don't move their HQ here!"

Chapter Twenty Seven

Little Scampering had another hero: Thomas Bowlman. Mind you, they weren't too bothered about the woman he'd saved. Serve her right, was the general opinion.

Belinda Thredsham claimed she had no intention of harming Sally, she just wanted to frighten her after all the distress the reporter had caused. Belinda and her partner, Donald Parkforth, had been looked upon with some pity following Sally's revelations and it had appeared they could re-build their lives in the village with a degree of local support.

But this act of unnecessary violence had undone the good work. There was no need for her actions and people started to wonder about having such an aggressive person in their midst. She was charged and would face the magistrates where, it was hoped, she might get another custodial sentence. Grace raised the point with Edith.

"Knowing courts today she'll get a slap on the wrist and be back here in no time. Anyone who annoys her could end up being threatened, Edith."

"Yes, I know, Grace. But to me there will always be the doubt about her intentions. Was she going to stab Sally? Who knows? But thank God for dear Thomas. I shall be sorry when he's finished here, and that'll be soon. I think that's quite enough violence for one lifetime. I shall be seeking peace and quiet from now on!"

Under her parents' guidance Alison quickly started divorce proceedings and put her house on the market. She'd move in with her parents.

"Sad really," mused Edith, "I liked her very much, and I think we could've made much of her garden, and it would've been the ideal therapy to get over her life with that awful man. But I can understand why she doesn't want to stay there."

"I agree, Edith," responded Grace, "she seemed a lovely girl and it'll take a lot to get over what she's been through. Out here in the country, well, that's perfect. But when you consider Little

Scampering is a place of murder and assault perhaps she's going about it the right way."

PC Thomas Bowlman was commended for his work that night, but Sally managed to make her front page article all about her, about how she was unafraid faced with her own certain death, about how she leaped at Belinda and held her legs while the officer handcuffed her. In fact, she made the whole incident into a tremendous drama in which she emerged as the heroine. Poor Thomas wasn't mentioned by name at all.

Another hero was Fido the dog. Loved wherever he went everyone would stop to pat and praise him, and his owner, Philip Plusmith, was enjoying a celebrity existence, enhanced by the increasing number of walks he and Fido took in the village. Welcome in the *Downsman* man and dog were worshipped with doggy treats always available, at least for Fido, although Philip preferred a pint.

***

The DCI and Willie Broughton were sharing a coffee in her office during a lull in their hectic timetable.

"Basically then, this goon assumes Mrs Footlong's identified him and makes the one mistake that catches him out. What a prize prat! But we're grateful for 'em, eh Willie? And I'm not sure we would've found it easy to progress this one, but thankfully we didn't charge Carl Merde."

"No ma'am, thank the Lord. And I do think we should be grateful for Mrs Footlong's efforts as she did lead us to the killer!"

"Be cautious with your gratitude there, my boy. She's an amateur sleuth and they are not my flavour of the month. And she got it wrong." There was a short-lived giggle on both sides.

"I don't know," Sheelagh said with resignation, "this was never going to be easy, no real clues, so maybe we needed divine intervention. Perhaps the gods sent us Edith Footlong! I don't know who sent us that ruddy woman from the paper. Blinking nuisance she turned out to be. Bowlman did well, even if he did recommend me to Mrs Footlong. I think the whole team has done well in what has been a truly challenging case. Yes, that includes you, Willie. Happily the killer gave himself away, but without that Bowlman wouldn't have been there to save Sally what's-her-name, and we'll never know if Belinda Thredneedle, or whatever her name is, intended to kill. So, we might've had two murders in Little Scampering! Bad for Kent tourism, that."

"And don't forget that Mrs Footlong was actually saved by a dog, because Digbin *did* intend to kill."

"True. Funny how the dog gets all the attention …."

"We're a nation of dog lovers, ma'am, and we especially love hero hounds."

"True again. Shame we can't always show such affection for those we love. Take poor Alison Digbin. How could she keep taking those beatings? I know, I know, it's not as easy as that, Willie, I know. But what possesses a bloke to keep doing that to someone he's supposed to love?"

"I understand that there are some women who beat their partners, ma'am, and I have no idea how anyone can hit the person they purport to love, I mean, inflict pain. How can you do that? And it's not just physical, is it? Mental and emotional assaults are just as bad. Male or female, it makes no difference, does it?"

"No Willie, it doesn't. Changing the subject a bit I did once give my partner, Katie, a spanking, but it was just for fun, she enthusiastically asked for it, and we both thoroughly enjoyed it." Willie looked aghast.

"Got yer going there, didn't I, Willie? And by the way Katie is dying to meet you. Fancy coming for dinner one evening? Bring Sian, and no, there's no talking shop." Willie was astounded and rendered speechless which caused Sheelagh to burst into laughter.

"Okay boy, I'll let you think on it! Don't worry, dinner only, no spankings …."

***

Fido had become friends with Jilly, the elderly corgi who was the true companion of Angela Compton, and Mrs Compton had therefore become friends with Fido's Philip Plusmith. Sadly, poor Jilly didn't get out much these days but did take a short stroll

155

in the village each day, and that is how she chanced upon the canine hero.

Angela was quite garrulous on the first real meeting, for she'd only ever been on occasional nodding terms with Philip as a fellow villager, and she wanted to know all about Fido's heroics.

"I'm afraid Jilly wouldn't be much good saving someone's life, but she could certainly bark at an assailant! But she's my best friend, well, dogs are, aren't they?" she chuckled, nervously. "I expect Fido's your best friend, Mr Plusmith."

"Yes indeed, and please call me Philip."

"Oh, so kind, and I'm Angela. I don't think we've ever spoken, have we, Philip, so it's so nice to chat to you and get to know Little Scampering's hero." Again she giggled, shyly. "You must be very proud of him, saving our dear Edith like that. Is he a good boy as a rule? I bet he's good company, particularly on your walks. Does he eat very much? My Jilly doesn't these days. Still, where would we be without them?" Philip was exhausted just listening, but talked quite freely and pleasantly, and gradually Angela relaxed and thereby stopped gabbling.

From that small beginning a new friendship was born and a few days later, early morning to avoid the heat, they embarked on a lovely walk atop the Downs, Philip, Fido and Angela. Jilly had been out even earlier and was content to sleep while her mistress departed for a short while.

Fido frolicked, and the two humans talked and admired the countryside as they went. They were not the sort of people who take the views for granted, so they made frequent stops on their way to enjoy the panorama, especially where they could see the Downs drop away before them.

"Isn't this spectacular, Philip? There must be so many folk in Kent who don't know countryside like this right on their doorstep. My late husband used to walk for miles up here, just to adore these scenic views. I accompanied him sometimes, but he was a keen hiker and used to stride out. Fit he was." Philip could sense sadness coming into her voice.

"If you don't mind me asking, Angela, did you lose your husband recently?"

"About six years ago. Wonderful man he was, and no, I don't mind you asking. He went out for one of his marathon treks and didn't come back." Philip detected a little gulp in her speech and knew the pain was there. "He was over at Charing somewhere, had a heart attack and died there. He was found on a footpath, probably too late to save him." And a small tear fell. Philip reached out and put his arm around her and she drew herself into his embrace and sobbed. "I'm so sorry, Philip ..."

"No, don't be. It's alright, it's alright." And he hugged her to him.

"I am sorry, behaving like this .... "

"There's no need, really there isn't." She disentangled herself, pulled out her hanky and tried a weak smile. "I know what it's like to lose someone precious, Angela."

"Oh Philip, I know so little about you. Have you been married?"

"Not married, no, but my partner died ten years back and he's been irreplaceable." He saw the look of surprise on Angela's face. "Yes, I'm gay. Do you mind?"

"No, of course not, I'm just very sorry for you, I mean, losing your partner. Was it sudden?"

"Almost. Cancer, you see. Diagnosed one day, three months later he's gone."

"Oh Philip, that's so awful. I'm so sorry."

They walked on, much to the delight of Fido who was missing attention, but they walked on arm in arm and in relative good cheer, kindred spirits in loss.

***

Quite by accident a little gathering of people was enjoying Edith's hospitality, primarily cold drinks but also some biscuits and some homemade date and walnut cake. Grace had met Poojah outside and the pair of them engaged the passing Nancy Harmand in conversation, whereupon Edith went out and invited them all in. They politely feigned reluctance but Edith's powers of persuasion won them over. Poojah was asking for their opinion on an idea she'd had.

"I did ponder the question of first aid. Do you think people might like me to do some very basic first aid training? You never know in this village when it's going to come in handy!" And they all laughed, but thought it a splendid concept. Of course, you couldn't keep chatter about recent events at bay, especially with Grace present.

"I was astonished about Mrs Thredsham, and I'm amazed she felt driven to such ends, but then we've never truly known her or Mr Parkforth. Mr Digbin is a different matter, and I'm not at all surprised. You can surely tell us all now, Edith, was he the culprit you told the police about?" Edith blushed.

"No he wasn't but the police have asked me not to reveal more information. I'm sure you'll understand." It was a huge fib but nobody looked as if they were sceptical. There was more general conversation about the crimes and the possible fate awaiting Mrs Thredsham, and then the nattering turned to current events.

"I suspect we all know who the new Prime Minister is going to be," Poojah remarked, "but will she make a good job of it? Times are really quite bad, aren't they?"

"Yes," said Grace, "and I've no idea who is on strike today …"

**

Lucy and Hassana were having a short break and sitting under a tree in a park. It offered precious little shelter from the heat despite they being out of the sun.

"How was it, y'know, interviewing Digbin? I could've killed him for the way he treated his wife."

"It was stomach churning, Hassana, and he was so vulgar with it. So brazen, well, so male, if you know what I mean. All so bloke-ish, but this wasn't banter, this was about the cold-blooded murder of a woman and the attempted murder of another. He was so detached from the horror of it. Talked about it like it was a minor offence, as if it was something that people do every day."

"Trouble is, Lucy, it *is* getting every day, isn't it? My sadness is that it's lost its power to shock, and that is what really gets to me."

"I know, Hassana. Still, it's up to us to do the best we can. Why we joined." And they sat and reflected on their own thoughts without another word until it was time to head to base where they found Willie looking very pale and staring into space.

158

"Wazza matter with you?" Lucy asked.

"Er ... er ... nothing. Just had one of those morale boosting meetings with our great leader ..."

"Blimey. What happened? Did she praise you, perchance?"

Willie was still stunned and struggling to come to terms with Sheelagh's revelations and invitation.

"Er ... er ... well, yes she did," was all he could manage.

"Hells bells, Willie. Must be a first!"

Chapter Twenty Eight

Carl Merde had been exonerated but was unforgiving. His younger son, Stephen, was told in no uncertain terms that he was well down the Christmas card list, and Carl was openly rude to villagers he knew had condemned him. With this action he lived down to his reputation for being obnoxious.

He did have time for Edith but he was a man possessed by bitterness and resentment, twin demons that, if allowed to flourish in his heart and mind, would devour him whole and ruin him. His conversations with Edith were thus stilted and laced with barely concealed aggression which Mrs Footlong did not find attractive. She started keeping her distance.

The immediate neighbours were made to suffer, as if they hadn't suffered enough from the Merdes. For example, he played the same songs over and over, very loudly, so that they radiated from his patio doors directly into the neighbours' gardens. One of these was 'Night and Day' which was heard on average once every thirty minutes.

He abused Francesca Towford in the street, referring crudely to her alter ego in a vile and obscene manner. She ignored him but was seething. When she reached home she deliberately broke five plates, two cups and four glasses, smashing them on the floor one by one while she damned Carl with similar language to his. It made her feel better, but she knew it couldn't go on.

And it wasn't going to. No sooner had he been cleared than a 'for sale' board went up and they knew they might well be rid of him. Surely they could tolerate his filth just a bit longer?

***

In time August became September and Britain's new Prime Minister was announced, not that it was a surprise to most who was chosen.

At long last the much needed, longed-for rain came and soaked everything, as is the way of things. And while one rain fell another reign was coming to an end. On Thursday the eighth the Queen died and it felt as if the world had ended. Grace watched the falling rain and remarked:

"Even the skies are crying their eyes out."

It was more than the end of an era, it was end of something very beautiful that many Britons loved but had assumed would always be there. Seventy years on the throne, coming to a sudden end. At least Her Majesty had been able to celebrate her Platinum Jubilee along with millions of loyal subjects, plus people all around the world who now mourned her.

There was disbelief and for many it took days to sink in. It really had happened.

The state funeral was on Monday the nineteenth and was a spectacle that only the British could stage. It attracted a worldwide audience. It was as fabulous as it was sad, the glory of British organisation and execution, now employed for one of the most sorrowful of occasions.

In Little Scampering feelings ran deep and many tears were shed. All the villagers watched the funeral and Edith had a house full, well, eight visitors to be precise, and she provided refreshments as you might imagine. It was still difficult to believe Her Majesty was gone. Even Jilly the corgi looked down in the mouth as if she sensed an affinity in grief with her canine pals seen at Windsor.

***

As Grace predicted Belinda Thredsham was dealt with leniently by the magistrates being handed a suspended sentence, much to everyones' chagrin. However, Falconwood Cottage was the next property on the market so another difficulty was going to be removed from the settlement. Belinda's plea, that she only intended to frighten Sally, was reluctantly accepted in the absence of any evidence to the contrary.

Sally Cainton did not reappear in the village, and, sadly, neither did PC Thomas Bowlman, his duties there complete. Edith had grown to love the young man and she sent him a special card wishing him well in his career. He wrote a touching reply and said he would keep in touch. Edith didn't doubt he meant it, and, anyway, she now had his home address!

161

Happily, the police presence vanished altogether, and most hoped it would never be needed again.

The Bargemans were pleased with their decision to stay especially now the more untidy elements were removing themselves. But there was fear of the unknown. Too many heading for their country escape were, to the Bargemans, unfamiliar with life out here and not keen to adapt to village life. They dreaded more Londoners coming for no other reason than if the Merdes were typical examples they didn't want to see the rest. Fortunately, the Merdes were the exception rather than the rule, and the Bargemans contented themselves with the view that they too had been incomers, escaping the urban world.

***

The summer appeared to be on the wane, with baking hot days gone for the time being. However, the Thracks' teenagers assured their parents it was a sign of things to come, and that excessively hot summers might be the order of the day. Why couldn't they wake up to the threat of climate change? Harry Thrack summed up his feelings in one line.

"Oh right then. Stand by for a soggy, wet summer in 2023! You wait and see."

"It's not about that, dad," his son advised, his voice full of frustration, "it's not about what happens next year, it's about what happens in years to come."

"And that'll probably explain why we're going to have a hard winter."

"Oh dad, for God's sake. You and mum, you're impossible!" Harry didn't help by laughing.

But it was cooling down now and the nights were drawing in, and at last the asthmatic Nancy Harmand was able to breathe easily again, much to Ken Waghorn's pleasure. Indeed, villagers generally were coming out more readily, and at all times of day, and for enthusiastic gardeners the rain had brought salvation, and with it the chance to get the gardens of Little Scampering up to speed.

The pub was still doing a roaring trade and once again customers were partaking of hot meals, particularly Sunday roasts. Thankfully, Felicity Trumpling was never revealed as Edith's number one suspect, although Edith herself remained puzzled by Felicity's knowledge of the position of the body. Peter Digbin rarely went to the *Downsman* so that aspect would forever be a mystery.

***

More rain came, but it was intermittent and there were still some warm days to be enjoyed as September handed over the reins to October. And it was in early October 2022 that the Little Scampering Residents Association and Neighbourhood Watch became a reality, with Mr Harper in the Chair, Mr Sonnel as Vice-Chair. Astonishingly perhaps, a very keen Francesca Towford was elected Treasurer, with other ladies ready to offer secretarial support to the group.

Edith smiled upon it all, not one for smugness, but she nonetheless exuded pride at her creation, and was notably proud when Francesca put her name forward and succeeded in gaining an important post. Good for us women to be represented at the top table, Edith mused. In fact, absolutely essential!

Poojah started her basic first aid courses with a good take up, and Edith proposed a gardening club which had not yet taken shape but was on the way.

Having approached a renowned local historian, Edith suggested that villagers be known as Scampers, this having some weird sort of historical association according to Roland, her esteemed guide. So Scampers it was.

***

Edith looked around her garden and thought about the shocking conditions the plants had put up with but acknowledged that she had a positive profusion of late autumn colour. The roses looked grand, the small red chrysanthemums were putting on a real show, the pretty pink nerines, on their tall slender stems, looked graceful and lovely, the variegated leaves on the geraniums were a sight to behold, as fine as the flowers themselves, the beautiful yellow blooms on the kerria were out in full, and there was a host of other colourful additions.

To one side were her reddish-brown sedums, just in front of a blaze of yellow and blue dahlias, and even the lawn was recovering.

She smiled to herself. My, she thought, it's as if the plants are showing me they've survived and are grandstanding, as she believed the word was. And they were! It was almost overwhelming for a keen gardener. All her efforts, including using her bathwater, had paid off.

And there was more joyous news to come, for her son and daughter had heard about the murder and then about their mother's brush with certain death, and both resolved to be over for Christmas. A beautiful outcome from something so hideous.

***

Willie Broughton finally bit the bullet and accepted Sheelagh's invitation on behalf of himself and a very startled DC Sian Stramer. But they had a most enjoyable evening, Katie's exceptional cooking skills producing a fantastic meal. And late evening Willie took Sian back to his place where they revelled in each others company, and then tucked into a terribly unhealthy breakfast before going to work. Another day, another dollar. Another day of crime for the police force.

And Little Scampering returned to as near normal as could be expected. Peace at last, but a community truly united.

Even if Grace Cathcart never knew who was on strike…. Or, for that matter, who was Prime Minister!

Author's Afterthoughts

This book was effectively written in 'real time' between June and October 2022. The heatwave and its effects in Kent and various other happenings described herein really occurred including, sadly, the death of Queen Elizabeth II.

The vague location of Little Scampering is deliberate, but the setting on the Kent Downs is very real, as are the descriptions of the views and the countryside that lie at the foot of those hills. There are many beautiful and scenic viewpoints along this escarpment all the way from the Medway to the east of Charing. Otherwise, this is, in all respects, a work of fiction.

The police officers, their ranks, procedures and behaviours are products of my imagination and exist to suit the story, and are no reflection on the real Kent Police.

Little Scampering is fictitious but there are villages of all shapes and sizes in the Kent countryside. The county is still remarkably rural despite urban development and you may stumble upon a Little Scampering anywhere. In my books that feature Kent I do my best to praise some of its finest features and delightfully attractive countryside. You will find references to Queen Down Warren, south-west of Sittingbourne, Crundale betwixt Canterbury and Ashford, Romney Marsh, the Alkham valley inland between Dover and Folkestone, the Weald, and the villages above the Kent Downs, to name but a few.

The list is endless. The county is surrounded on three sides by water (ideal for de-salination plants, since we're short of the stuff) and there is an astonishing array of coastal scenery and coastal towns and villages too.

***

During August 2022 I stayed at the Chilston Park hotel and sampled the Afternoon Tea. In fact, the meals were superb, the staff friendly and efficient, and the rooms excellent. A beautiful escape in lovely surroundings. Sadly, my favourite B&B in the county, Brambles at Eythorne, is no more. Praised to the heavens in *Death at the Oast*, it has closed for good and I feel as if I have lost a good friend!

After three murder mysteries in the Kent countryside I think it is time to base one in neighbouring East Sussex, an area I think of as a sister to my own county. We have much in common, not least plenty of glorious unspoilt natural beauty and charming villages. The more I think about it the more I am convinced and I shall apply myself to it at once!

If you haven't read *The Chortleford Mystery* and *Death at the Oast,* and you've enjoyed this one, do please try the forerunners. One reviewer likened them to 'Midsomer Murders comes to Kent' which is a good compliment I should think.

Explainers

As I seem to have a small following in the USA and Australia I'll add some explainers just in case readers there are unfamiliar.

AONB – Area of Outstanding Natural Beauty. Land protected by the Countryside and Rights of Way Act, aiming to conserve and enhance the natural beauty and environment. The Kent Downs is one of over 40 in the UK.

DWP – The government's Department for Work and Pensions.

NHS – our National Health Service.

Other books by Peter Chegwidden
(those marked # available Kindle only)

New work coming soon (2023):

THE VALOUR OF THE HEART
A moving story of love, heartbreak, sacrifice and hope
As a young teenager a determined Enid Campton has her life mapped out. She will become a secretary until she marries childhood sweetheart Micky Bowen and then she will become a mother.

However, 1939 brings war and Enid's life changes forever. Micky joins the army and she enlists in the ATS. Then news arrives that Micky is missing, presumably killed in action. She keeps her dreams alive but as time passes hope fades. She meets a seemingly kind man and love grows, and they marry after the war, only for Micky to arrive home from Japan where he has been a prisoner. Heartbroken, Enid realises it is too late.

Her husband is revealed as a womaniser who uses brutal violence too readily. With Micky now married all she has left are her two young daughters and she resolves she will be strong for them, ensuring they have happy childhoods, and in devoting herself to them she will make something of her own life despite her loveless and unhappy marriage. She will never lose her love for Micky.

But there is a terrible tragedy and some serious shocks in store for Enid.

Meanwhile Micky makes the most of his own life, never quite free of his love for her.

On occasion fate plays a hand and their paths cross. But life has a way of delivering joy and misery in unequal quantities, and happiness and grief befall both Enid and Micky as the years go by. Could they eventually be re-united or is their love for each other doomed?

***

Author's comment:

This story is largely based in South Woodford on the border between east London and Essex, an area I grew up in during the fifties, sixties and seventies, the period in which the tale is set, and I have drawn on many personal memories. Most of the places mentioned are real or at least existed at that time. During the war my father was a prisoner in Japan and my mother was in the ATS, but the principal characters are not based upon them although some of their wartime recollections have been employed in the story. My family have their roots not far from Woodford in East Ham, Forest Gate, Manor Park and so on, and again I have used family wartime and peacetime reminiscences in the early part of the book. Many real events are also incorporated as the account develops.

***

Murder mysteries based in the Kent countryside

- The Chortleford Mystery
- Death at the Oast

"The Chortleford Mystery" – a lovely old gentleman is slain in his back garden and the villagers guessed who the killer was, his wicked stepson. So why weren't the police doing anything? Gossip takes hold, an investigative local reporter gets involved, and then another murder takes place. Gradually secrets are uncovered as the police dig deeper into the crimes, secrets some wish to be left buried from view. And it is only a matter of time before a third murder takes place.

"Death at the Oast" – Sunday morning and Audrey Modlum has been playing golf, and returns home to find her husband stabbed to death in the hall of their converted oast house. DCI Sheelagh Mehedren has little to go on and then octogenarian Ernest Pawden, a fan of crime novels and TV crime shows, gets involved and gets in her way. But his own investigative work uncovers vital clues, yet places a lovely old lady's life in peril.

Crime novels

- No Shelter for the Wicked
- Deadened Pain #

"Deadened Pain" is a parody of the crime genre featuring a most unlikely police force trying to solve a series of murders. Occasionally humorous, often satirical, there are also serious messages amidst the pathos and poignancy as this bungling outfit tries its best and frequently falls short.

"No Shelter for the Wicked" follows the fortunes of a new private detective, David Canbown, as he finds himself caught up

in a murder investigation. He becomes a suspect in one of the four killings initially baffling the police, and gradually becomes more deeply involved especially when other private eyes are drawn into events. The trail leads from Kent to Hertfordshire, Suffolk, north Devon, Derbyshire and Cumbria where Canbown faces a life-or-death situation. In the meantime he has been helping a young woman try and locate her long-lost sister, a quest that also proves hazardous.

Historical Novels (based in Kent)

- Kindale
- The Master of Downsland

"Kindale" charts the adventures of a mysterious man, Oliver Kindale, who is clearly on a mission. It is the late 18th century and with Napoleon rising to power in France the fear of invasion is real. Kindale arrives in Kent and is interested in a notorious Frenchman living under an assumed name in Dover, and in a rogue highwayman noted for his power and violence. The two men could be connected which, to Kindale, points to a serious plot afoot with the country likely to be in jeopardy.

"The Master of Downsland" concerns a man who is disinherited for marrying the girl he loves and who therefore leaves behind a life of high status and wealth to make his own fortune. David Grayan succeeds and eventually he and his wife, Marie, take on a large estate in north Kent. True philanthropists they employ many more than they need to, provide the local village with a hospital and school, and care for the local people earning their respect. Then Marie dies in childbirth and David is bereft, retreating into a world of self-imposed darkness and suffering, which even his close friends cannot relieve. Then a new maid starts at Downsland. But could a lowly servant provide any medium by which he could emerge from gloom, and could he love again? This is a story of love, tragedy and bigotry set against society's conventions in the late 18th century.

Adventures of Tom the Cat

- Tom Investigates
- Tom Vanishes #

A couple of lovely cat stories for adults! Not cartoon or any sort of animated cats but the real cats we see around our neighbourhoods, behaving just as we see them. But in these tales (tails?) we are allowed into their world, and learn what they are thinking and saying. These two books are about a series of adventures surrounding a tabby called Tom and his friends, and are great fun. So get in touch with your feline side and come along for the ride!

Short Story Collections

- Sheppey Short Stories #
- Souls Down the River

"Sheppey Short Stories" – 18 tales of all kinds, all based on Kent's Isle of Sheppey. Humour, pathos, poignancy, satire, and a little sauce too.

"Souls Down the River" – a glorious romp down the imaginary Flemm Valley somewhere in the English Countryside. The journey pauses in each village to enjoy a tale or two, tales of sauciness and frivolity, of muddle and mayhem, of romps, scandal and rustic charm, all stories told with warmth and humour and without malice or unhappy endings. Here's a couple as a taster. We take up the perambulation in the hamlet of Bordham Witless where Emmeline Munch is travelling on the local minibus, operated by Oliver Buckett:

Bordham Witlass

Emmeline Munch wasn't the only passenger, the other one being out of sight on the floor. Her faithful Collie bearing the name Fetchit went everywhere with her.

170

An octogenarian, she lived with Fetchit at Little Pryck, and travelled to Bordham Witlass to collect her pension at the post office. She did not have a bus pass and paid her fare in cash determined to ensure her details never appeared on any computer. "You'll never find me on one of those damned computers," she'd once told Oliver, "as they are the instrument of the devil himself." Oliver had smiled to himself knowing full well she was on more computer bases than she could ever imagine. Local council and state pension just for starters!

She also had no time for men. She could think of no reason why such horrible, useless creatures should exist at all, and felt that women could get by comfortably without them. Obviously she had not stopped to wonder how her mother had given birth to nine children, possibly believing pregnancy was a simple act of nature that occurred anyway.

Emmeline was born in a disgusting hovel in Oddchester before the second world war. It was soon after the Depression but her father was lucky to have work on the railways where he was a fireman. It had probably not occurred to her that her papa was a useful male since his work produced the only income they had and they all had to live on it.

She was the sixth child and now she had outlived all her siblings. Her father died in the war; although he was in a reserved occupation firing the engines he was sadly a victim of a bombing raid which destroyed much of a depot, his locomotive included.

Gradually the family's fortunes improved, Emmeline herself taking on employment as a maid, and soon after the war they were able to move into better accommodation. In time, as the need for maids decreased, she became a live-in companion to an old housebound lady, and then continued in service as a lady-who-does, doing domestic cleaning work and other duties. When she retired she and her mother decamped the big city and headed for the hills and the fresh air, finding a decent cottage in Little Pryck that was entirely to their liking, and there they stayed until her mama passed away a few years ago. Thinking she might like to return to what she called civilisation Emmeline looked at urban properties in Great Barsterd, but soon discovered the town wasn't worth a light and remained at the cottage and acquired a dog for good measure.

Fetchit proved a successful hound when it came being good company and a good guard dog, but had a propensity for finding things before they were lost. On one occasion, when the pair were out for a walk in the valley, Fetchit sprinted for a small thicket on some pretext or other, disappeared for a few seconds, whereupon there was a feminine squeal and a masculine cry of "get off", and the dog promptly came racing back with a pair of knickers and a pair of pants in its mouth.

Woman and dog now made their way into the Post Office.

That the PO survived at all in such a tiny hamlet in this day and age was down to two things. It was the only one in the valley and there was a public outcry when closure was proposed, and it was also a book shop that sold a few pharmaceutical items as well, a hardware store, a pet and horse supplies centre, and a farm shop which ensured its viability.

The Postmistress, Penelope Podium, watched Miss Munch and Fetchit approach the counter, knowing what the answer to her first question would be.

"How much Miss Munch?"

"All of it."

Her pension was counted and handed over, Emmeline moving on to the book department. The assistant there, Jackie Crumpton, took a step back and spoke.

"Don't come too near Miss Munch, I've got the snivellums."

"Snivellums? What's they?"

"Well I'm sniffing and sneezing and probably got a cold coming."

"Get that tin of liniment over there and rub your chest. It's big enough."

"My chest?"

"The tin."

Jackie took another step back.

"Besides missy you shouldn't be at work if you're not healthy." Jackie ignored her by changing the subject.

"Oh, we've got the latest Maggie Hope in. Would you like a copy?"

"Yes please, but tell me where, don't want your germs."

She was directed accordingly. Miss Crumpton had often wondered why a woman who didn't think men needed to exist at all found pleasure reading what were, to some degree, romantic novels. Maybe they reflected a love long lost, or perhaps the books had taken the place of men in Miss Munch's life.

Having made her purchase which included two other paperbacks Emmeline brought Fetchit round to the pet section. She enquired of the dog whether he wanted this or that, bought what she believed the collie had approved, and headed for the farm shop.

The owner of the entire emporium, Douglas Mintpick, was there to greet her.

"Lovely to see you again, Miss Munch. Hope you're well."

"Reasonably well disposed Mr Mintpick, and Fetchit is fine as you can see. But Miss Crumpton shouldn't be here; she's sick."

"Thank you Miss Munch, I'll send her home shortly." And with that busied himself sorting some potatoes out.

Having bought some eggs and vegetables and a bottle of apple juice purporting to come from Flemmdale (she knew of no orchard or individual apple trees) she asked Mr Mintpick if he knew what time Oliver Buckett would be back from Great Barsterd. They had this conversation every time. Since nobody knew what Mr Buckett was up to and where it was a pointless question.

But there was purpose to the request.

"Don't worry Miss Munch, I'll drive you home in the van when you're ready."

"Thank you Mr Mintpick, that's so kind."

There, he thought, I'm another useful male. See?

Miss Munch's views on the opposite sex were well known everywhere. The dialogue about the mini-bus cropped up every visit and always had the same result, a lift home for Emmeline and Fetchit.

Today, by chance, there was a variation.

Mr Mintpick put her purchases safely in the back of his van while she climbed into the passenger seat, then he held the back door open for the dog. But Fetchit barked twice, suddenly scampered across the road and leaped a stone wall.

"Ye gods," cried Douglas, "what's got into him?"

"What's happened? What's up Mr Mintpick?"

"Miss Munch, I'm sorry but Fetchit has just shot off over that wall there," he explained pointing in a vague direction. Emmeline muttered and accepted assistance back out of the van and began calling. Barks could be heard in the distance but of Fetchit there was no sign.

The two humans went over to the wall and called out but all they received were barks in reply. Then Fetchit appeared close to the river bank barking some more. But he would not come back despite his owner calling him a naughty boy who wouldn't get any treats later.

"What are we to do Miss Munch?" a despairing Douglas Mintpick asked. Just then Jackie Crumpton appeared on the scene enduring a particularly hearty attack of the snivellums.

"Ish trine t' tell ush sumshing," she cried through her hanky. Mintpick was good at translating snivellage into English. He explained to an exasperated Emmeline.

"Jackie says he's trying to tell us something. I think she means we need to go to him rather than get him to come to us." Jackie was nodding furiously.

"Well, one of you go then. Whatever next." Upon this matronly command Jackie looked at Douglas and he at her and Jackie decided she'd just been elected to carry out the task.

"Take my mobile Jackie. Just in case." He handed his phone over and a cold feeling flowed through her. He's had a premonition, she reasoned, and grabbed the mobile, climbed over a gate and dashed across the field towards Fetchit taking her snivellums with her.

Girl and dog vanished.

Then Penelope Podium came trotting out full of disorder.

"Douglas, it's Jackie on the phone. There's a young child down there, fallen in the river, numb with the cold and wet, and she's trapped under a branch and she's in danger of drowning."

"Tell her I'm coming and call an ambulance Penny. Grab some blankets, towels, anything like that and put the kettle on, and start a fire somewhere." With that he climbed the gate, caught his foot and fell headlong into the field.

"Oh f-f-f-f-f…."

"*Mister Mintpick*, please, there's no need for language," cried a shocked Emmeline, "and do get a move on." He picked himself up and did as he was bid.

By the time he'd reached the riverside Jackie, up to her waist in the water, was supporting the sobbing girl and keeping her safe. Douglas weighed up the situation and hurling himself into the river managed to move the branch that was causing the trouble and Jackie was able to lift her onto the bank.

He took the child in his arms and ran up towards the post office, passing her over the wall to Penny Podium who wrapped her in blankets and took her to the rear office where Jake Throwby, seconded from the pet shop, had lit the wood burner.

The women looked after the stricken, frightened girl and were able to extract her name and address but not her phone number. Douglas recognised both surname and address, checked his customer list and phoned her parents in Sawe Bottom. They arrived about the same time as the paramedic and about ten minutes before the ambulance.

Katy, for that was her name, recovered her spirits and went to hospital for a check-up where she was pronounced to in perfect working order and was taken home by her parents.

The eight-year-old been playing with two friends but they had lost her and she had walked for miles down the riverside until, exhausted, she fell in. Weakened, she could only make pitiful noises but Fetchit had heard them.

Needless to say Fetchit was the toast of Flemmdale and promised a medal by the grateful parents. He seemed much happier with the doggy-chews they bought him. Jackie's immersion appeared to have cured her snivellums, or at least they were easily forgotten. She and Douglas were hailed as the human heroes but, being self-effacing they said it was all down to the dog, which up to a point was completely true.

Eventually, having changed his soaking wet clothes and dried himself, Douglas was able to take Emmeline home. Outside her abode she turned to him and spoke.

"Mr Mintpick. You were wonderful. You got everything organised as you shot off to the rescue and not only did you do well saving her, you came flying back with her so the ladies could tend her. Then you notified her parents. I must say, Mr Mintpick, you are a credit to your sex, and I have never had cause to say that to any man. A credit, Mr Mintpick, a credit."

He sat back with a smile on his face. Coming from Emmeline Munch they were quite the most special words he could've heard. He took the shopping to her door, as well as a bag of doggy-goodies that everyone present had chipped in for, and then they both stood aside as a guard of honour as the true hero trotted up the path and into his home to a round of applause.

Well done Fetchit!

And on along the valley to the village of Lower Down:

Lower Down

Maisie lived in a short row of pretty cottages in the hamlet. To one side of the terrace was another B & B which was not as popular as Dale View but which was usually busy enough during the summer, and at the opposite end of the terrace was a peculiar looking conglomeration of buildings belonging to the brothers Tom and Mike Flowers.

Tom was the motor mechanic and part of the site was dedicated to his calling, boasting a couple of workshops, one of which was fully equipped to carry out MOTs, a pokey little office awash with paperwork, and a small store for parts. Tom's part of the enterprise was well guarded, with gates, a state-of-the-art security system, and a high fence topped with barbed-wire. The man himself was relatively lithe, athletic in build, exuding fitness.

This was in contrast to his brother Mike who ran a butcher's shop, and looked every inch the quintessential vision of a butcher, being portly, hearty and full of good humour, and always wearing the butcher's apron and a straw hat to complete the picture. He cheeked his customers and they loved him for it. The shop also sold the type of groceries, such as tinned food and frozen items the Florist and Mr Mintpick's farm shop didn't.

His home-made pies were the toast of Flemmdale. His sausages were renowned all over Countryshire. At times his shop throbbed with clients, locals and tourists alike, and there were times when there was a queue outside. To help him he had Bobby

McQueen (known as Steve for obvious reasons), his own father (who had retired but couldn't give up), and a young couple from the village, Nancy Albright and Willie Darke who were very keen on each other but too shy to proceed.

Mike's wife, Shirley, and his mother also gave a hand when necessary. It was actually Shirley who made most of the famous pies.

After Tom was born his mother longed for a girl but got Mike instead and was so disappointed she dressed him as a girl for a couple of years, an action that earned him his nickname Rosie which had stuck ever since and which he clearly loved. Rosie Flowers was adored everywhere.

In complete contrast Tom was the quiet one, as yet unwed, who went about his business uttering few words and rarely laughing or even smiling. He serviced most of the vehicles in the area and had plenty of work given some of the cars were positively ancient. He'd tried to give up on Ollie's minibus but Mr Buckett looked so heartbroken when Tom informed him that he relented and continued to fight with it, somehow keeping it on the road.

Today, during a lull in early morning trade, Mike was looking at Nancy and Willie who were busy but managing to find time to glance at each other, the glanced-at looking away at once as soon as the glancer's eyes made contact. Gawd, thought Mike, what a pair of virgins. And what names: Albright and Darke. Blimey. He and Shirley had tried from time to time to encourage the pair but realised they were just too shy. If only, Mike had concluded, more young people could be like that!

Neither had any sort of mobile phone. In his spare time Willie walked the dale, while Nancy would set up her easel wherever the fancy took her and start to paint exercising no skill or sense of artistry whatsoever. Mike had even spoken to their parents on the QT but all four had given up hope, exasperated. Indoors Nancy would read books or draw, and Willie would listen to classical music or enjoy a chat with his dad. They couldn't be encouraged to show an interest in anything else.

It was known that, out on his lengthy walks, Willie often bumped into Nancy who would be busy painting, especially along the river, but any dialogue was assumed to be brief and of no consequence.

However, unbeknown to all and sundry, Nancy and Willie were no shy virgins. Far from it. When they met in the valley it was by arrangement, and although much of the dialogue might indeed have been brief and inconsequential, the action was fiery and red hot.

Of course, they could hardly go to their bedrooms in their parents' homes for such pleasures.

And while Mike and co watched out for their coy glances in the shop they were missing what the hands were up to. Nancy had a way of manipulating a large sausage that could bring Willie to the boil, and he in turn could fire up Nancy by very gently squeezing a chicken breast in a suggestive manner.

It was little wonder her paintings were rubbish. They were a cover story. In their bedrooms they would write extensive love letters and surreptitiously hand them over at work. They often snatched a snog in the cold store and it's amazing they didn't defrost all the frozen meat. When the weather was unsuitable for meeting outdoors they contented themselves with writing love notes the length of novels. Or reading the letters they'd recently exchanged.

Willie had a ground sheet and towels in his back pack, and Nancy's painting gear also housed vital equipment for their combined leisure pursuits. Thus was all concealed from a pack of adults who couldn't see past the obvious.

Today, their lunchbreak was going to be rather different. Nancy's father had gone to work and her mother had joined two friends on a shopping raid in Great Barsterd, travelling by taxi. She and Willie were going to share a bed, her bed, for the first time. So excited was she that she suggested to her lover they try and get the afternoon off so they could liberally extend their hour until the likely arrival time of mumsie, possibly around 3 p.m. Asking Mike at different times, and knowing the shop would not be too busy, their efforts were rewarded without Mike considering their requests suspicious.

By a quarter past twelve they were on the bed letting fly.

Now, if the course of true love does not always run smoothly, the course of deception can be stormy, so there was consternation

178

and blind panic when mumsie turned up just after two. They had to make decisions in split seconds and one of the more bizarre ones led to Willie being bundled out of the window onto the flat roof of the conservatory below, his clothes being bundled after him while Nancy hastily dressed indoors.

Her mother was surprised to find her home but accepted her explanation about having the afternoon off as the shop was quiet. Then there was a shriek and a cry of 'Oh bugger' emanating from the garden. The women rushed to the rear where mumsie was treated to the sight of a naked Willie sprawled in her azaleas.

"Oh Willie, Willie," squealed his beloved, who was no more aghast than her mother who threw her hands to her face then screamed 'Oh God' several times. Willie had unbalanced himself trying to dance into his underpants, the difficulties faced by many a man struggling to dress in the morning, and fell off the conservatory breaking his fall on the plants but luckily breaking no bones.

He was led inside, mumsie covering his nether region with a tea-towel, and given medical attention for a few cuts and bruises while Nancy went upstairs to retrieve the rest of his clothes. Once good order was restored it was time for the three of them to sit in the lounge and for the inquest to begin.

But mumsie started by delivering a surprise.

"Look, you're nineteen Nancy, and Willie you're twenty-one. You don't have to hide. I'd rather you didn't go to bed together in my home, but there is no need for deception. I trust you're taking precautions?"

"Yes mum, I'm on the pill."

"Well, thank God for that. It seems just about everybody has been hoping you'd get together. Not least me and your dad, and your parents too Willie. I don't approve, but you must have enough money for a night in a hotel or something. I take it this was the first time?" They both blushed, silently unveiling the truth, which in itself was a lie of course.

"Oh dear me. Well, as long as you've taken precautions at least that's one worry we haven't got. But why the deception?" It was Willie who answered.

"To tell the truth the more people wanted us to be an item the funnier it got. We've just played it along for a laugh, like, but we'd have told you eventually. Just having a laugh Mrs Albright, that was all."

"That was a laugh today wasn't it Willie? You'd have been in stitches alright if you'd hurt yourself badly. You might have had broken bones to contend with, you young fool. And you young lady, I'd have expected better of you. All I ask now is that you both forget to mention it to your father because he won't see the funny side, believe me. Let's just keep mum, eh?" Both nodded.

If Mrs Albright had been given a shock, then up at the garage Tom Flowers was also in for one.

He dreaded seeing Hortense Winders draw up in her Fiesta. A single lady, of very appreciable wealth, she'd bought an old farm house near the village and made a good fist of doing it up tastefully. Or at least her contractors had. She moved in and found herself attracting the attention of young males lacking her financial prosperity. Those she fancied, and frankly that was most of them, she allowed closer inspection of her fifty-seven-year-old body, dumping them as soon as they had given their all.

She knew they were after her money, but she made the most of their efforts, enjoying every moment and lapping up the intimacy, the cat with the cream.

But it was a different matter when it came to trying to land a more permanent fish, and right now Tom Flowers was in her sights. If she'd had asdic it would've been a case of 'instantaneous echo'.

The problem was that she really had no idea how to woo a man and tended to coarseness of expression when addressing Tom, her lecherous leer only adding to the man's dismay and dreariness. Today was no exception.

"Tom, it's about time you got your hands on my big end," followed soon afterwards by "I expect you've got a really firm crankshaft." Her risqué double-entendres were lost on Tom and this afternoon he'd had enough of her. He led her into his office and sat her down unaware her excitement was increasing, or that he was going to seriously disappoint her.

"Hortense, thank you for all the business you give me. It is really appreciated. And you have recommended me and that has brought even more business. I cannot tell you how grateful I am. But, please forgive me, I am going to be blunt with you. There is

180

nothing wrong with your car. You look after it, drive it well and, excuse my self-praise, with my servicing it should need little attention. Anybody can check your tyre pressures, your gardener for example.

"But you are such a good customer I don't really mind how often you call, but I beg you, I plead with you, stop these silly remarks you make. I don't find them amusing and, in my opinion, they belittle a fine lady as I am sure you are......" The words died on his lips as Hortense burst into tears and buried her face in her hands. Such action was wasted as Tom had never been one to react to a woman in tears, and he simply rose and walked out the office, whereupon Miss Winders dried her eyes and sat there looking perplexed. Eventually she stormed out after him and found him underneath a Focus.

"Come out of there this minute Tom, I want to talk to you."

"No you don't, you want to shout at me and tear me to pieces and I'm too busy."

"Come out here Tom, or I'll drag you out by the feet."

"That's assault."

"Fine. You can call the police while I talk to you. But I am not having a conversation with the front of a Ford Focus. I want to talk to you now. Not to shout, not to grumble, but to thank you for your honesty. Perhaps it's what I needed, a verbal spanking."

There was a pause then slowly Tom emerged.

He remained on the ground where he pulled himself into a sitting position and drew up his knees.

"Talk then. You've got two minutes."

"Only need one. I apologise but I thought I was amusing you in a sort of bloke-ish way, the way I imagined you men liked. I'm sorry, but thank you for your honesty, and for not taking any notice of my tears. I deserve far worse for being a stupid woman. At my age I should know better. You've been cruel to be kind and I will come to appreciate it. Well, that's my minute up. I'll be off now." And she turned and headed for her car without a backward glance.

Mmmm, thought Tom, that cost her, but maybe she'll be off my back now. Bloody woman.

At that precise second her car made a horrid metallic noise and came to a sudden halt. Tom walked over and looked down at the driver. She had an air of resignation about her as she glanced at him.

"Now then Miss Winders, sounds bad, would you like me to take a look? If I can't do anything right away I'll run you home." Hortense tried a wan smile, nodded in an almost subservient way and sighed as her eyes searched the ground in front of him.

"Thank you Mr Flowers. We understand each other. That's a very kind gesture. "Not at all Miss Winders. You're one of my best customers after all."

She climbed out of the car, humbled but in a strange way very happy.

Tom's assistant, Barry, helped push the Fiesta into the garage. Then Tom came across to Hortense.

"On reflection, no point looking now and keeping you waiting. I'll drive you home Miss Winders." "Thank you Mr Flowers. Is it serious do you think?"

He paused, deep in thought, then replied.

"Could be your big end needs seeing to........."

Printed in Great Britain
by Amazon

22038708R00106